T0367376

PAYBACK

BY:

G. T. ENGELKE

authorHOUSE®

AuthorHouse™
1663 Liberty Drive
Bloomington, IN 47403
www.authorhouse.com
Phone: 1-800-839-8640

First published by AuthorHouse 3/7/2011

ISBN: 9-781-4567-1943-2 (e)
ISBN: 9-781-4567-1944-9 (sc)

Printed in the United States of America

Ryan, Rebecca, his family and the men and women of his Precinct have their wits tested time after time.

With a killer that seems to be intent on killing half of the people in the city by himself. One at a time, His 'How' is ingenious and his 'Purpose' is an intense one, with no limit.

A brazen thief, a local thief, a thief that flaunts his crimes because it is all about being proud of showing absolutely no fear of capture or remorse.

Brothers that do not know what it is like to have any feelings of remorse, nor do they want to know. No matter who gets hurt or shows up dead. People are expendable to reach ones goal.

A Terrorist threat that could change the world forever, it could also be the first step that leads to the end of the word as we know it.

Chapter 1

---

*R*YAN PULLED HIS CAR INTO the parking space that was always open for him, directly in front of the luncheonette's door, and after putting it in park and turning it off, sat there for a moment watching the activities through the windows.

The parking space was always open due to the sign that the local police precinct station had put up years before. It stated, Reserved for Lieutenant William Ryan. Violators will be arrested and given 30 days interment in New York State enforcement facilities. Ryan had had a TV News Crew's van towed from a crime scene and the crew running down the street after the van had been shown on another station's news report that night, much to the delight of the First Responders that have to put up with the news media and the circus they bring with them on every call they pick up on their police band radios.

He watched as Lynn moved from table to table with a pot of coffee toping off each customer's cup. He also saw Catherine moving from the kitchen pass through with plates stacked up her arm towards a table with four men sitting at it. From their dress he made them to be construction workers, 'Pipefitters' from the look of their colorful skullcaps. At Five A.M. almost all of the luncheonette's patrons would be blue-collar workers, some going on and others getting off shift. Reaching for the car's door handle he stopped cold. His glance had caught the movement of the door opening that led to the restrooms and the person that stepped into the room looked very out of place. The man was about six feet, with very black hair, and dressed in a light tan three-piece suit. Everyone in the place had turned to watch the man as he made his way towards the booths that lined the rear wall. Ryan's glance scanned the booths on the rear wall and he did not see anything on the tables. That and the fact that everyone had stopped and turned to watch the man's movements made him reason that the man was just entering the luncheonette. He knew that one could enter from the alley next to the luncheonette and then enter the main room from the hall that the restrooms were on. Ryan watched as Lynn moved towards the booth that the man had selected to sit in and reaching it she placed a napkin and set of silverware in front of him. He sat so that he could see all that entered and exited the front door while also having a view of the door he had entered through.

Ryan got out of his car still watching the events unfolding in front of him. It appeared that Lynn had gotten the man's order and was walking back to the kitchen pass through to place it. She looked at Catherine and rolled her eyes mouthing what he thought was "Trouble." Catherine finished placing the plates of food that she was carrying in front of the men seated at the table. She then moved over to where Lynn was standing and they exchanged a few words.

Walking briskly Ryan reached the door and pulled it open. The bell that hung on the spring wire clattered announcing his entrance. He walked normally back towards the last booth, and reaching it sat facing the man's back. To the casual onlooker it appeared that man had not even looked up.

Ryan slid his revolver out of its holster and placed it on the seat next to him. His entrance seemed to break the spell that had set in over everyone when the other man had entered. Catherine moved over to his booth and asked a little louder than required, "What can I get you?"

Ryan grinned and replied, "The usual."

As he was replying she placed an order slip on the table. It read, "He's packing."

Ryan nodded.

Catherine moved towards the pass through and without thinking yelled his order out as she had done a hundred times before, "One Ryan's Special." She never thought to order a Taylor Ham with a fried egg on a hard roll with a side of home fried potatoes, crisp, any other way.

Ryan saw the man sit up very straight and, from the slight dip in his shoulder, reach into his jacket. Ryan had his gun on his lap as he watched the man slowly step out of the booth and turn towards him. The man's hand was still in his jacket and it never moved as the man walked towards Ryan's booth. The man stopped just across the table from Ryan and with a smile on his face asked, "Ryan, Detective William Ryan?"

Looking up, Ryan replied, "Yes, and you are?"

The man asked, "May I sit?" without an answer to the question asked.

"Yes," Ryan replied

Without removing his hand from inside his jacket the man slid into the booth.

Ryan spoke quickly but quietly saying, "I hope whatever it is that you have in your hand doesn't cost you more than you can pay my friend."

The man seemed to freeze for a second then replied, "I will remove my hand very slowly and place what I hold on the table." With that the man removed his hand from his jacket and placed what he was holding in front of Ryan.

Ryan looked at the black velvet bag and said without thinking, "What in the hell?"

The man slid out of the booth saying, "It is from your Uncle in Sicily, I was instructed to give it to you and only you. He will contact you." With that he turned and walked towards the door. He dropped a twenty-dollar bill on the table that he had been sitting at as he passed by. In a moment he was gone all that was left was the clatter of the bell. A feeling of ease seemed to fill the room.

Ryan picked up the black velvet bag and looked at the red pull strings that held it closed. The strings were held in place by a gold clasp with the letters 'VB' pressed into it. Picking it up he was quite surprised at its weight, he fingered the gold clasp he put the bag into his pocket just before Catherine returned to the table with his order.

"What was all of that?" She asked. Sounding relived that the man was gone.

"Something, something that proves that there are just too many people, people that know when and where I am."

She grinned, not fully understanding what he meant, but having an idea. "Stuff happens."

"Yes, yes it does and at the strangest times. By the way, thanks for the heads up." With that he picked up the cup of coffee and sipped it but not tasting it.

She replied, "Any time" as she walked away.

He slid his pistol back into the holster when it seemed most appropriate to do without being noticed. He would open the bag when he was alone. Funny but it seemed to be warm, even through the pocket lining and his shirt. "Stuff Happens," he thought as he finished his breakfast.

After paying for his breakfast, and kidding with Catherine and Lynn for a few moments walked out to his car. He had just gotten his seatbelt connected when his phone began to buzz and vibrate. Pulling it out of its holder he flipped it open and was surprised to see "Caller blocked" displayed on the back lit screen. Pushing the ANS button he said, "Ryan."

"Billy, Vincent, please take very good care of the object that you were given, it dates back many centuries. You will receive instructions soon that will help protect you, yours and our family. It is very important that you don't open the package until you have heard from me again." The line went dead.

"What the hell is that about?" Ryan sat there looking at his phone, he murmured to himself, "A strange bag, a call from halfway around the world and I still don't have a clue as to what it is all about. And how in the hell did he know that I just left the luncheonette?" That question was answered as he watched a black Hummer pull away from the curb, make a U-turn and head up town, in his rear view mirror. Shaking his head and grinning he started the car and headed for the precinct house.

Chapter 2

---

*R*YAN AND *G*RAVES REWOUND THE security tape for the tenth or eleventh time. Graves pushed the Play button and with out looking away from the screen said, "It's like he was wearing gloves, but there are no gloves. Lou, He's not wearing gloves, damn it, why the hell aren't there prints all over that room?"

Ryan shook his head replying, "I just don't know, it doesn't add up. He wore a mask, sunglasses, scarf, and plastic bags over his shoes. He worked real hard not to leave anything showing that could be traced but kept his hands uncovered. He kept his hands bare knowing that he wouldn't leave prints. Hell of a trick."

Graves shook his head, "Not that he just didn't leave prints, he didn't even leave smudges. If he burned his fingers smooth with acid, or something, there would still be smudges left by the oil on his skin."

Ryan pushed away from the desk saying, "You are completely correct but if he's wearing something over his hands it's invisible." Standing and walking towards the door he continued, "Let's take a break from this for a while. I've got a mound of reports to finish and so do you."

Looking up Graves replied, "You're the boss."

"Right." With that Ryan walked down the hall to his office, entered and sat at his desk. He thought about the tape and the tapes from four other crime scenes, and how each had shown the "Perp" with everything covered but his hands. He realized that the "Perp" was having a good time making them look foolish. They had scoured each crime scene for the most minute object, and come up empty.

Shaking his head he picked up a few of the papers lying scattered there and started to sort them by importance and due times. His cell phone began to beep. Taking it off of his belt he flipped it open and seeing the display that read SLIM, pushed the green highlighted button, with the miniature phone glowing. He smiled "Ryan, and what did I do to deserve this call Pretty Lady?"

With a laugh in her voice Mrs. Rebecca Ryan replied, "It's not what you did but what you're going to do, Mister."

"Is that a promise or a threat my dear?"

"It's a promise in both the way you are thinking and the reason I called."

"Ok, you have me. What's up?"

Rebecca laughed, "You bet I do, buddy. The reason I called is to let you know that were going to meet Danny and Maria and Kenny and Sue for dinner at eight tonight."

"That sounds good to me. Is it any special occasion?"

"I don't think so; at least Maria didn't mention anything. My guess is we just haven't seen Maria and

Danny for a while and it's been a long time since we've seen Sue and Kenny."

"Ok, I should be home around 6:30. See you then. Love You."

"Love you." The line went silent.

He thought about how long it had been since he and Rebecca had seen his cousin Danny and his wife Maria and surprisingly it had been over two months. Just living only an hour apart didn't seem to matter, they never seemed to get together more than three or four times a year. That is unless a case came up that they had to work on together. Danny's promotion to Detective Sergeant specializing in homicide cases, in the Borough of Richmond, had increased that opportunity significantly. He was looking forward to seeing his cousin Kenny again; it had been a few years since the last time they had gotten together in Florida just before he moved to Las Vegas. His cousin Kenny had recently married Sue and moved back to the area from Las Vegas where he had met and married her. He had worked for the last two years, as the manager of the city's bus and monorail maintenance department and the MIT had made him and offer he couldn't refuse. Glancing down at the remaining papers on his desk he semi grunted thinking, "Well, they won't go away by themselves."

He spent the next few hours reading reports, jotting notes on each, and after placing each in a department envelope and writing the destination across the front, put them in his outbox. The stack in his outbox grew, and before he realized the time, Graves took a half step into his office saying, "Five thirty, see you in the AM, Lou."

Ryan looked up and replied, "You bet, didn't notice

the time. Let the Desk Sergeant know that I'm going to be up here for another half hour or so."

"You got it."

With that Graves turned and walked away.

Ryan pushed a few buttons on his cell phone so that it would ring in thirty minutes just to prevent his being late and not getting home on time.

Turning back to the remaining reports he picked up a Five and just had begun to read it when he heard, "Have a good evening Lou." Looking up he saw Malone looking in his doorway and with a wave she was gone. The thought of "Wonder how come she's been so quiet lately," passed through his mind.

The word "Busy" and then quickly "Sorry" followed from down the hall.

He grinned and shook his head saying out loud, "I think that I need to talk to her tomorrow."

Leaving the building and walking towards the subway entrance Malone caught herself looking over her shoulder once again, "Damn it, there's nothing there."

But the feeling was still there, it felt like bugs crawling, moving back and forth, over her skull. It was hard not to reach up and scratch her head raw.

She stared at the sidewalk about four feet in front of her as she walked a little faster. She tried to concentrate and read the thoughts around her but all she could get was a jumble, a jumble that had no beginning, nor end. She took the stairs down to the station and as she stepped lower and lower the feeling subsided just a bit.

This was the second day that the feeling bombarded her mind, it started yesterday the moment she stepped off of the subway. The feeling stayed with her until she closed the door of her apartment and it only happened on the way home and not a thing on the way to the job or anywhere else. When it left it was like a weight was suddenly lifted off of her mind and the clarity that followed was startling. Her mind felt new, as strange as it sounded to her it felt like her mind was cleaned. Her gift of being able to read people's minds felt stronger than ever before.

Chapter 3

AFTER ARRIVING HOME HE PLACED the black bag into the wall safe that held all of their important papers and the good pieces of jewelry that Rebecca had inherited and the few he had given her. Their discussion about the bag was short, just the mention of his Uncle's name was answer enough for Rebecca right now.

After cleaning up and changing they had a glass of wine and briefly each went over how their day had gone. At seven twenty they left the apartment and walked to the garage and Ryan's Vet. Ryan and Rebecca drove over to 4th Street Station to meet Danny, Maria, Kenny and Sue at 'The Shamrock Inn.' Rebecca explained how the vote was five to one for an Irish dinner over and Italian one. Ryan laughed and said, "I don't remember voting." Rebecca grinned replying, "You did via an absentee ballot that we filled out for you. We knew if you got into the discussion we'd be eating pasta again."

Ryan laughed saying, "You guys are tough, out voted without a vote."

"Right," Rebecca replied as they pulled into a space in front of the Inn.

She looked at Ryan and said, "I just don't know how you do that."

Ryan looked at her saying "What?" as he opened the car door.

"In a city with over ten million people you pull up and there is always a parking spot open and waiting for you right in front."

Ryan opened the car door for Rebecca as he replied, "Just lucky I guess."

She grinned replying, "Right."

As they entered the main dining room they saw their family sitting at a corner table. Danny looked up and waved. Once at the table they all hugged and kissed their hello's and it's so good to see you, in true Italian fashion. Ryan and Rebecca took the two empty seats and were not surprised to find their drink of choice waiting for them.

Danny looking at Rebecca said, 'We've ordered some appetizers and they should be out soon."

Rebecca smiled and replied, "Wonderful."

The waitress appeared as if on queue and places three plates on the table. Smiling she said, "I'll be back in a while to check on you and take your orders for dinner."

"Thank you Cathy," Danny replied as she turned and walked away.

Ryan took one of the Scottish Eggs, one of the grilled bangers and one of the deep fried stuffed potatoes from the plates Cathy had set on the table. He placed the plate in front of Rebecca trying not to disturb her conversation with Sue. He then repeated the process for himself, Danny and Kenny did the same.

They were enjoying the appetizers, drinks and company trying to catch up on all that had passed since their last meeting and the men were talking work and the ladies sharing just good old information.

Kenny's wife Sue was talking with Maria about the problems in keeping Kenny's uniforms looking respectable with all the grease, and all that he works around. Maria replied, "The towels must be the worst, I know that between Danny and the kids, towels are my biggest problem." Looking at Danny with a grin she continued with, "The towels seem to catch more dirt than the soap."

Sue laughed a little saying, "That used to be a big problem but Kenny uses those spray gloves now when ever he is going to work with the wrenches again and the grease just washes off his hands like magic."

Ryan overhearing Sue's comment looked at his cousin's wife exclaiming, "That's it. That's it."

Danny, Maria, Rebecca, Kenny and Sue looked at him with a surprised, and a questioning expression on their faces.

Ryan looked at them with a blank look for a moment until he realized that they had no idea of what he was talking about. He grinned and explained, "Sorry, it's just that Sue's mentioning of spray gloves may have solved a question that has been driving my detectives and me crazy for a few weeks. I really can't get in to it right now but that information will be a really big help."

Sue blushed a little.

Seeing how uncomfortable Sue was with the attention Rebecca quipped, "Then I guess dinner is on New York's finest."

The rest all laughingly agreed.

Ryan picked up his glass and toasted them with,

"Ok, dinner is on me." Leaning towards Rebecca he continued with, "I mean us."

They all laughed, and reaching towards the center of the table they all clinked their glasses.

Cathy returned and took their food orders and requests for drink refills.

Chapter 4

*R*YAN LEANED CLOSER TO *G*RAVES as they looked at the tapes of the robberies again saying, "He had his hands sprayed with those liquid gloves. You know, like the spray stuff mechanics use to keep the grease off their hands." Stopping the tape he tapped the screen saying, "I didn't notice the slight sheen that is reflecting off of his hands before."

Graves leaned closer and murmured, "Ain't that a bitch." He leaned back and looking at Ryan continued with, "I wonder what is left when you remove that stuff, for that matter, how do you remove it?

Ryan leaned back replying, "Well, you can use a solvent or, depending on how much you sprayed on, you can peel it off. I've been told that the best way is to peel it off and then use a cleaner on your hands."

Graves said grinning, "Peel it off. Bet that leaves prints, if not prints, DNA. I guess it's time to check the area outside of the locations of the robberies and see if any skin was left behind." He stood and glancing at the screen again shook his head mumbling, "That is one cocky son-of-a-bitch."

Ryan stood replying, "Yes he is, get a few uniforms and have them check all of the gutters, garbage cans and parking lots in a four block area of each crime scene. This guy wouldn't be rushing when he left."

"You got it, Lou."

Chapter 5

RYAN WALKED ALONG HOUSTON STREET, not really seeing, but seeing, each one of the people that seemed to swarm in all direction around him, towards the Deli that his Cousin Danny had picked to meet for lunch. He was pondering Danny's voice mail that he had received earlier that morning. It was short and to the point, "Hi Billy, Danny, Meet me at Jerry's Jewish Deli at 11:45 for lunch, I'll buy." Try as he may he just couldn't piece anything together. He was not aware of anything going on in the family or for that matter, anything outside of the normal daily madness that is New York. He had just seen Danny and his wife Maria three nights ago when he and Rebecca had met them for dinner. All seemed well at that time. He stepped around two young women that stopped in the middle of the sidewalk to look at what looked like a theater time schedule. Just as he cleared them he saw Danny walking through the door of Jerry's Deli a half a block ahead of him. He picked up his pace and reached the door in just a few moments. Glancing around the room he saw Danny being seated in the rear corner of the room. He walked towards the table observing each person at the other tables without even knowing that he was doing so.

Danny looked up and seeing Ryan smiled, and speaking loud enough for Ryan to hear, told the waitress, "I'd watch this guy. He looks like trouble to me."

She looked Ryan up and down and with a big grin she replied, "He sure does. Think he'd mind coming home with me so that I could find out just how big a trouble he is?"

Before Danny could answer Ryan pulled out a chair and as he sat said, "Sorry good looking but I've never been able to finish anything that this guy starts. And I'm sure that of our wives would agree."

She laughed and replied, "Dam, the good looking ones are always married. Would you like coffee or coke?"

They both order a diet Pepsi.

"Got it," and with a wink she walked off.

"How is Rebecca?"

"She is well, were driving out to Long Island Saturday to visit a friend of hers to pick up three or four textbooks that she needs for a class she is taking. Maria?"

"She is well also, the kids keep her busy."

Ryan looked at his cousin and cutting to the quick asked, "So what's up, you sure didn't say anything the other night at dinner and not much in the voice mail you left. Is it something in the family or work?"

"No, no, I just need to tell you something before it gets announced. I'm leaving the department."

Ryan leaned back in his chair with a look of surprise on his face and after a few seconds had passed replied, "Okay, what's the story? You just don't leave the department after twelve years of service and a promotion to Detective Sergeant. Are you in trouble?"

"No, it's nothing like that," Danny replied. He continued, saying, "I was picked by a new Federal department to run their operation, it's based on the west side of the island in Prince's Bay. From there we'll be covering the entire Northeast. They're crediting me with all of my time, towards all benefits, and a pretty healthy salary increase. With the new job I'll have the same authority as a Federal Marshall."

Ryan leaned across the table and in a lower voice asked, "Federal Marshall, damn that's strong. Is it about drugs?"

"No, I'm sure that at times it probably will be related but I will not be on the streets at all."

"What is it that you'll be doing?"

"Well the Department is FETOC."

"FETOC, what the hell is that?"

Danny grinned saying, "Yep, FETOC, it stands for The Federal Electronic Tracking of Cash. We're looking for the illegal transfer of large amounts of cash from drug sales, robberies and that kind of stuff."

Ryan leaned back in his chair smiling and saying, "You sure you know what you're getting into? Those drug guys really don't like when you mess with their money."

"Yep, the department has been in operation in a few test areas for the past few years, and with 90% completion of the monitoring equipment being installed, the remaining three operation centers are being placed in the "Go Mode."

"Monitoring equipment?"

Before Danny could reply the waitress moved to

the table and placed their drinks down asking, "Know what you're having?"

Danny replied, "I'll have a corn beef on rye, with mustard, Jerry's salad, and a kosher pickle."

She smiled saying, "Got it." She turned looking at Ryan asking, "And you, trouble?"

Ryan smiled back replying, "Hot Pastrami and the same as the rest of his."

"Be about ten minute's." She walked away and stopped after a few steps and looked back to see if they were watching her walk away, they were. "Okay?" she asked.

Danny answered, "One of the best walk aways I've seen in a long time."

"Thanks," She smiled and continued towards the kitchen.

Grinning Danny shook his head and looking back at Ryan continued, "Over the past four years FETOC has been working with the Department of Federal Highways installing monitors in sections of every major highway in this country. Every fifty miles or so, and at each exit and on ramp in the cities, eight foot sections of the highway were removed and new concrete installed. The monitors are buried in the new pours and send out signals that are picked up by a special set of satellites that have been put in place from the space station that floats up above us. That information is then sent to the four operation centers' computers for interpretation and action."

"Satellites, space station, operation centers, you're pulling my chain, right?"

Danny laughed, "No, It's hard to believe but FETOC's operation is but a small part of what those satellites are there for. Were kind of an added benefit, or to be more truthful a second thought."

Ryan leaned forward again saying, "Okay, so you've got this monitoring equipment and satellites. Just what are you monitoring?"

Danny leaned closer and replied, "Money. We can tell how much money, down to twenty dollars if needed, is in any vehicle that goes over any one of the monitoring stations and track where it entered a highway and where it exits. Of course we have the monitors set at the ten thousand dollar level most of the time."

Ryan shook his head saying, "I knew those chips that they started to put in bills years ago were going to be used for something. How many people are driving around with ten grand in their car?"

Danny laughed replying, "Way more then you would ever believe, way more."

The waitress moved to the table and placed their platters in front of them saying, "I'll be right back with some more drinks."

They both said "Thank You."

She smiled and said, "Manners too, I should be so lucky."

The three of them laughed as she walked away.

Ryan and Danny ate their sandwiches enjoying each and every bite. Ryan did not know what he enjoyed more, the sandwich or Jerry's salad. The salad was slices of crisp cabbage soaked with a blend of oil, vinegar and spices and refrigerated for at least twelve hours before serving. Once they finished their sandwiches Danny continued, "Do you remember the small town in West Virginia that had those two highway vehicle stops on the interstate that resulted in the recovery of over two million dollars in drug monies last year?"

"Sure. That was FETOC?"

"Yes, that was one of the test sites; another is on the southern part of US 95 South."

"Every fifty miles of interstate, that cousin, is one hell of a network, when are you going to start?"

Danny laughed, "Last week, the official paper work will read that I've left the department for a private business venture. They are attempting to keep this whole thing under cover for as long as possible. So, this lunch never happened."

As if on cue, the waitress stepped to the table and holding the two checks in her hand asked, "Okay, who's the lucky one?"

Danny reached for the checks smiling, and saying, "Well I've got the lunch so I guess he's got the tip."

Ryan glanced at the check he could see and the total due was nineteen fifty said, "Done." He placed a ten-dollar bill in the waitress' hand saying, "Enjoyed the lunch and the service."

They both left with a "Thank you, come again" following them out the door.

Stopping on the sidewalk, a short distance from Jerry's doorway, Ryan faced his cousin and shaking his hand said, "Best lunch I've had in awhile and the very best of luck Cousin. If I can ever help I'm just a phone call away."

"I know that and thank you. Give my best to Rebecca."

"And you to Maria."

With a wave they headed in opposite directions.

Chapter 6

AT THE SAME TIME, JUST blocks away, Danny and Ryan's Uncles, Sal and Big Frank, stood close together speaking in very soft voices, the traffic sounds drowning out their words, assuring them that they could not be overheard. Even if a directional listening device was being used. Their lives were full of always having the possibly of one Federal Department or another trying to record anything and everything that they said.

They spoke into each other's ear and after five or six minutes passed they shook hands and started to walk in different directions.

Sal pulled his hand out of his pocket to signal a cab to take him back to the ferry terminal to travel back to Staten Island and home, and as he raised it, a young lady passing by pointed at the sidewalk and said, "Sir, Sir you just dropped a dime."

Sal laughed softly as he leaned over to pick it up replying, "Yes, Yes your correct, Thank you."

Chapter 7

BARRY WHITMORE WALKED OUT OF his place of employment promptly at 4:33 PM, after punching out. He looked back at the building and shaking his head said out loud, to no one but the wind in his face, "Another day another dollar." He enjoyed his job, most of the time, and even liked his boss, most of the time. He knew that he was one of the best contract proofreaders employed by Data Check Ltd. Spending eight hours a day reading contracts and checking them against original documents wasn't a bad way to make twenty-nine fifty an hour. He smiled when the thought of the five thousand-dollar bonus he had gotten when he found where one of the contracts had been changed. His boss had asked him to clean up a few contracts that had been checked by a co-worker that hadn't shown up, one Monday unexpectedly, for work. If the contract had been counter signed and returned, as is, the company would have lost tens of thousands of dollars.

The smile on his face faded as he watched the security guard drive through the parking lot that his employer and the company next door shared. The security guards were always fucking with him, his car, and in his opinion, his life. He watched as the security guard stopped the car behind his Chevy. The guard got out and walked slowly around his car and with the chalk stick he carried putting a wide pink strip on each tire. The guard knew that this infuriated Barry. Barry picked up his pace while yelling, "Hey 'Rent a Cop' just what the hell are you doing?" The guard turned to look at him as he got back into the security car and yelled back, "Just making sure that you can find this piece of crap in a crowd." Pulling away just as Barry got with in ten feet of the car, the guard put his hand out the window and waved.

Barry watched the car turn onto the street and disappear in traffic. "Well enjoy it while you can. My day is almost here and all you ass holes will pay." Barry opened the trunk and took out the spray container of tire cleaner and as rag and cleaned each tire in turn. When he was finished wiping the tires he put the container of tire cleaner back in the trunk and picked up the tube of hand cleaner that lay next to it. Flipping the top of the cleaner open he squeezed a small amount into his hands and rubbed it in, rolling his hands as a surgeon would before an operation. Satisfied with his tires, and hands, his put everything back in its place and closed the trunk. As he moved around the car checking for any dings or dents he caught a glimpse of two of the other security guards standing on the loading dock of High Tech Printing Inc., the building next door, looking at him and laughing. "Laugh you bastards, soon I'll be the one laughing." His frustration level was so high that he was perspiring. His car was a 56 Chevy, about 80% original equipment and restored to street factory condition. The only thing that needed to be done to make it showroom quality was a new paint job. Barry refused to have this done for he knew that the car would then standout even more than it now did, and be remembered where ever he went. That was something that he just did not need.

On his way home Barry stopped at 'Making Stuff Inc.' to see if his order had come in. Much to his delight his order was in and waiting. The counter man placed the package on the counter and asked, "Cash, check or charge Mr. Jeffrey?" Barry placed two fifty-dollar bills on the counter and reached over and pulled the package over to his side of the counter with out replying. The clerk placed the bills in the register and gave Barry his four dollars and seven cents change. Barry muttered a "Thanks" as he stuffed the bills in his pocket and with his package under his arm turned and walked out of the door. He turned left and walked the block and a half to his car. His car was his only indulgence, very few New Yorkers put up with the expense and hassle of car ownership. He had made sure that he parked facing away from the store so that he wouldn't have to drive past the store windows. It wouldn't be good if the clerk just happened to look up and see him driving by. He had to be just a passing customer. This had been the fifth time he had purchased the items he needed and this was the fifth place he purchased it from, with every purchase under a different name. One just couldn't be careful enough.

It took him about twenty minutes to reach his home by car instead of the ten minutes by subway. Home, a thirty-one hundred square foot area on the first floor of a six story building built in Nineteen Eighteen. The building was one of three identical buildings that had been in his family from that time. He was the last of the Whitmore line and he had no intention of trying to extend it. In the Forties all of the wiring and plumbing was installed, as an after thought, with the wire and pipes run exposed. Two of the buildings had been converted into storage units of various sizes and he collected the rents via a mail drop. An agent rented the units and kept up with all of the nonsense that went along with rental property. The building he called home was empty except for his flat, workroom and the roll up door that allowed him to park off of the street. The flat only had two rooms and a bath but covered thirty one hundred square feet and he used all of the space.

He pushed the button on the remote that controlled the roll up door and watched the door start to disappear into the darkness of the space. When the door was half way open the motion detectors picked up the movement and the lights came on, all that was visible was black walls, but if the interior of the rest of the floor could be seen the lighting of the interior was brighter than daylight. Anyone looking in would first notice the cleanliness of everything. It was clean to the point of excess. For that matter each and every square inch of the buildings interior had been stripped of everything down to the bare walls, floor and ceiling. On each floor Barry had painted every inch with high gloss white enamel. On the floor he called home he had painted it with many different whites and the floors were covered with bright red carpet or tile. In direct contrast, the furniture was all black, and the windows were all covered with black paint. All of the lighting, heating and air conditioning systems, for each area, were controlled by motion and heat detectors, allowing him to sleep without being uncomfortable.

Once leaving the car with his package under his arm, Barry pressed the large red button next to the door into the living area. This closed and locked the roll up door and also put the motion detectors on line that surrounded each exterior opening on the ground level of the building's exterior. With that done he hurried over to the door that led to his work area that he had set up towards the rear of the floor. He opened the door and stepped into the room, the lights came on and he glanced around his area of discovery, as he called it. The computer-operated oven and walk in glassed door freezer, stainless steel tables and roller trays all glinted of cleanliness. It had taken him many hours, and days to find, install and place in operation all of the equipment in this room without leaving a single trace of where it came from or where it went. With all of the bar coding and computer tracking now being used on everything one purchases now, this was an amazing feat. He removed the item he had purchased and opening the oven door and placed it on the middle rack. Moving over to the P/C he typed in his instructions and hit ENTER. With this done he moved into the living area of the flat towards the half - walled area that his called his bedroom. The only areas with full walls and that could not be seen from any place in the flat were the toilet and the work areas.

He cleaned up, changed clothes and pulled on a pair of ultra soft boots with rubber heels and soles. He then moved to the kitchen area and made himself a sandwich of liverwurst and sliced onions on rye bread. This he devoured greedily with a cold beer. All of the time watching the white hands on the large black faced clock move ever so slowly onward. He heard a low buzz, that intermittently sounded, that came from the work area. He placed the plate he was holding in the sink and moved quickly to the work area's door.

Entering he hurried over to the oven and watched the timer count down to zero, the display read, COOL DOWN 5:00. The numbers began to decrease 4:59, 4:58, 4:57….. at 0:00 he opened the oven door.

Barry removed the rack that held the twenty four-inch plastic tube from the oven and placed it on a wooden cooling rack that sat on one of the rolling stainless steel trays. Moving the tray over to the refrigerator, that stood next to the sink he opened the refrigerator door and removed a tray that held layers of damp cool towels. He then placed a damp cool towel over the tube to cool the plastic so that he could handle it freely. If done correctly he would have ten to fifteen minutes to work with it before it shrunk and hardened. He touched the tube and felt that it was now workable so he moved it to the hard flat surface of the butcher block. Using the heel of his hand he pressed the tube into a flat oval.

Turning he picked up the short sword that he had set on the table earlier with his left hand and then with the can of "Pam" in his right hand sprayed the sword making sure to coat it completely.

With that completed he slowly inserted the tip of the short sword into the tube while pressing even harder on the tube with his other hand. Once the sword was inserted completely he then began to mold the plastic along the entire length of the blade with a small hard rubber roller using extreme care, insuring that the plastic mirrored the blade of the short sword perfectly. The roller would ensure that there were no air bubbles that would or could cause an imperfection. He widened the base of the mold, around the handle, to a three by three-inch square that was two inches thick. He could feel the plastic tightening and becoming rigid. He had timed it right and in another few moments the plastic would shrink, and set, causing its interior to be a mirror image of the sword's blade.

He wiped the entire mold down with another cool towel, and then another, making sure that it was completely cool to the touch.

He had tried other sizes and shapes of sword and each had failed. This was his eighth attempt at creating the perfect killing tool. This one would be perfect, because it was totally functional and completely untraceable.

"Ah, Done," Barry murmured as he moved over to the other table in the room holding the mold, still wrapped in a cool towel. Taking hold of the sword's handle he gently pulled it, while pulling the other way on the mold. The sword slid out of the mold with little resistance. Grinning he picked up the can of "Pam" and sprayed the interior of the mold again until he had a drip of the liquid fall from the opening. He held the mold by the tip end and swung the mold back and forth causing any excess lubricant to be expelled. With that done he carefully moved to the freezer and placed the mold on one of the holders he had attached to its inside wall. With that completed he filled the mold with distilled water from one of the gallon jugs stacked in boxes next to the freezer and closed the top. Each bottle of water had been purchased at different times, stores and outlets.

He stepped out of the freezer and closed the door. Looking through the door's glass he admired his creation saying, "Well, well, soon the testing will begin again."

It had taken him months of rummaging through

flea markets and antique stores to find the perfect size and shape sword. Some proved to be to long and thin while others to wide and bulky. He just knew that this one, yes this one, would be perfect, just perfect.

With all he could now do, done. He moved around slowly cleaning everything he had used or touched. He then moved into the living area and continued cleaning everything he had used or touched there. Once he was finished to his satisfaction he decided to go out for the few things that were still on his need to get list. After pulling on his coat he moved over to the door and removed the list from the tablet that hung next to his phone. With a glance towards the freezer he grinned murmuring "Soon." He opened the door and felt more than saw the lights go off as he left.

Barry walked to the subway entrance and took the next train to the Upper East Side. He entered a small butcher shop and waited for his turn at the counter. When asked, "What may I get you?" He looked at his list, just as any good servant would do, and responded, "We need two ten pound roasts of beef. Please make sure there is good marbling." Turning slightly away from the counter he said, "To lean and it will be dry." He said it as to himself but just loud enough to be heard by the other shoppers. He could see them nodding their agreement. The butcher glanced his way with a look of disdain thinking, "A day servant questioning his work, how absurd."

Once he paid for the roasts with small bills, and a sidelong look at the butcher, Barry placed the roasts into the large canvas sack that he had brought with him, the sack with the markings of a small shop in Long Island City. He walked out of the shop and walked north for two blocks before crossing the street and entering the subway station entrance.

The trip home seemed to take forever, the tunnel walls that normally flashed by, seemed to be creeping by at a snails pace. This of course was just his mind playing tricks on him. When the train stopped at his station it was all he could do not to run to his door. But at last.... he was home.

Chapter 8

FTER REMOVING THE COVER AND storing it in the trunk and putting the top down, Ryan backed the "Vet" out of the parking space and pulled up to the walkway that led from the stairwell. Just as he stopped Rebecca stepped out of the doorway with a picnic basket in her hand and a big smile on her face. Ryan got out and moved around the car to open the door. He took the basket from her and placed it on the rear seat.

"Thank You, things like that will get you everywhere."

"Promises, promises" Ryan replied, with a twinkle in his eye and voice.

They both laughed as she got in and put on her seat belt. He moved around to the driver side and getting in also put on his seatbelt. He leaned over and gave Rebecca a kiss saying, "This should be fun, been a while since we got away from it all for a bit."

She nodded and replied, "Yes, it has."

They were both looking forward to a day out of the city and the visit to the beaches of the island. Ryan was also looking forward to driving the "Vet" at something more than city speeds; he did not get the opportunity often.

It wasn't long and he was pulling onto the Island Expressway, shifting into third he pressed the accelerator about half way down and the "Vet" jumped up to sixty five before he left the entrance ramp. He slid it into fourth gear and backed off the gas but the "Vet" still leaped up to eighty five, he backed off the petal a bit more and brought the speed back to between sixty and sixty five.

Rebecca's hair flowed in the wind and she started to laugh, for it felt so good. "Oh Bill, I've missed this, it has been a long time."

Ryan just smiled and concentrated on keeping the "Vet" somewhere under eighty and enjoying every minute of the drive. They had been driving for about a half hour when his cell phone began to ring and vibrate.

He said "Damn" as he pulled it off of his belt. Glancing at it he saw that there was no number displayed on the screen. He pushed the send button and said, "Ryan."

"Cousin, Danny, I hope you are enjoying the drive. Just wanted to say 'Hello' and I hope the four thirty five you have and the three sixty seven Rebecca has gets you through the day. Be safe."

"Okay, I'm impressed, thanks. My best, home." He heard a double click.

Rebecca looked over as he was putting the phone back, smiling he said "Danny, I'll tell you later."

She mouth "Okay."

He thought about it for a moment before remembering he had mentioned the drive when they had been having lunch. His cousin did not miss much. It was a trait that seemed to run in the family.

They drive for about another half hour before turning off the expressway. It took another forty minutes to get to the little village that was there destination. The village was very similar to many of the villages that dotted the east and west shores of the Island. The business areas were old and comfortable with an easy feeling as you passed from shop to shop and the smell of the salt water sharpen your appetite a bit earlier than normal. It seemed like ever fourth or fifth shop served the food specialties of one country or another, with a seafood shop advertising local specials evenly scattered amongst them.

"Slim, where were we going to meet Karla?"

"I told her to meet us at that small park down next to the pavilion on the beach. We have about a half hour before we are to meet."

Ryan pointed to the seafood shop on the corner saying, "How about a few clams on the half shell for an appetizer?"

She grinned at him replying, "A few? A few dozen maybe, if it's up to you. Sounds good let's do it."

Ryan placed his hand on her arm and steered her towards the shops entrance saying, "Well, let's make the most of the half hour we have."

They sat by the window and after placing the picnic basket on the floor next to his feet Ryan order two dozen cherrystones on the half shell and two diet Pepsi's.

The waitress came back and placed on the table the two drinks and a condiment tray with a red cocktail sauce, horseradish and a bottle of onion hot sauce. There was also a small basket filled with packages of saltine crackers. She explained that the onion hot sauce was a local concoction that really gave the clams a special kick.

Slim opened one of the packets of saltines and put some of the onion hot sauce on each and handing Ryan one said, "Well, when in France."

He took a bite, not knowing just what to expect, and the flavor and heat jumped out at him. The heat was hot but not so hot that it overpowered your taste sensors and the onion flavor very mild and pleasant. He could tell that both would only enhance the enjoyment of the clams. He smiled and nodded to Slim and she returned his smile and said, "Nice."

The waitress moved back to the table and placed a platter of clams in front of both of them saying, "Enjoy."

Slim put a little of each of the condiments on the clams, she did so that she would have one of each in turn so that all of the flavors would be blended evenly.

Ryan covered each of the clams with some horseradish and put the red cocktail sauce on six and the onion sauce on the other six. He then put the cocktail sauce on four of the saltines.

Slim watched him and grinned, clams on the half shell was one of the few foods that Bill really enjoyed. It seemed that they only had them three or four times a year for some reason but each time was an event.

They finished and leaving the money with the bill on the table moved towards the door saying "Thanks" to the waitress as they left.

It took them just a few moments to walk to the park and they picked one of the tables with a great view of the pier and beach. Slim opened the basket and set out three places and put the two food containers that contained fresh cut Italian cold cuts and three types of cheese in the center. Bill sliced the round loaf of bread and placed the slices on the plate Slim had put out for it. He opened the containers of fried peppers, olive mix, caramelized onions and scooped them on the small condiment plates.

A pleasant voice said, "Don't spill any of that, Buddy."

He and Slim looked up to see Karla about five or six feet away. She already had her arms out to give Slim a hug. They all exchanged hugs and pleasantries and took seats around the table. Karla looked at the table and laughing said, "I'm starved."

They all made a sandwich and took some of the condiments, they each had a tall cold beer that Bill had gotten from one of the vendors that moved back and forth along the pier and pavilion.

The talked for what seemed like a few moments but after glancing at her watch Karla said, "Oh my, it's almost five o'clock. Bill you always distract me to no end, Rebecca keep a good eye on him or I'll do my best to steal him."

Slim, smiled looking from Karla to Bill and replied, "As you know, you cannot keep anything that does not want to be kept."

Karla let out a loud laugh and Bill put both hands up saying, "How did I get in the middle of that?"

Karla stood and began helping Slim putting everything away while saying, "Just wanted you to know how easy it is to get someone in trouble."

"Thanks."

Slim put the last item in the basket and Bill walked over and dropped the trash into the litter basket. Stepping back to the table area they all exchanged hugs and promises of getting together more frequently. They parted and Bill and Rebecca walked back to their car.

Their ride back into the city was uneventful and Slim fell asleep about ten minutes into the trip. Ryan mused, "The salt air had taken its toll."

Chapter 9

REBECCA STOOD OVER THE COOLER drawer looking down at the young body that lay there, holding the toxicological report that had just come back from the Lab. The report gave up nothing; there were no drugs, no poisons, nothing.

"Another twenty something 'Jane Doe,' that has recently given birth, dead. No baby, no after birth, no tearing, no signs of a struggle, everything nice and neat, just nothing out of place. It just does not make any sense, none at all."

This was the fourth such case in less than twenty or so months that had passed over her table, of a young woman found dead in an alley. With all signs pointing to a drug overdose being the cause, but no signs that any kind of drugs had ever been used before the final dose. No signs of physical abuse, slavery or prostitution, nothing, she was just dead. The kind of case that just sticks in your mind, sticks there and you can't shake it.

As in the other cases there were no next of kin

found and no hits on finger prints or DNA, just another of the cities ghost population, gone.

Rebecca had sent a request to all of the five boroughs medical examiners requesting any information on similar cases in their jurisdictions. All she could do now is wait, wait for them to respond, and she would bring the matter to Bill's attention.

Chapter 10

O PENING THE FREEZER DOOR BARRY lifted the mold off of the hanger and placed it on the tray next to the door. He held the mold with the open frozen end down and gently shook it while keeping his other hand at the opening. With just a few shakes the ice sword slid out of the mold and into his hand. Barry grinned as he placed it into the "Freezesac" bag that he had ready and zipped it closed. With the sword in the bag he walked over to the table and carefully placed it down.

He than walked to the other table and began phase two of his testing, Barry slowly stretched the one-eighth thick leather sheet tightly across the framing square and tightened the thumbscrews on all four sides. Checking to make sure that it was firmly pressed against the ten pound roast and the layer of quarter inch by one-inch hardened wood strips that were wedged in the vise bolted to his workbench. He flicked his finger into the leather and it gave a soft thump. "Perfect, that should give the same resistance as skin and bone." He looked around and seeing everything was in place walked back into the living area to occupy him for an hour or so.

He walked over to the table, putting on the deer skin gloves he carried looped over his belt, and put his hand on the cooler bag with 'Freezesac' printed on it in bold red letters. Looking at it he smiles and said to himself, "Wonder what the 'Freezesac' people would think if they knew their commercial really worked for me." The 'Freezesac' was perfect, just perfect for his needs. It was made for carrying six cans of beer or soft drinks, stacked on top of each other, by a strap that hung on your shoulder, much like a rifle would but hanging the opposite way. The manufacturer advertised its performance in commercials with a tall blond, in an almost non-existent bathing suit with a "Freezesac" hanging from her shoulder, standing in what appears to be a desert. With the sun beating down she wipes' her forehead with the back of her hand, and smiling at the camera says "I've been here for hours and it's time for a cool one." She opens the zipper of her 'Freezesac' and as she is taking out a can it starts to snow. She looks at the camera with a sexy grin, shivers and says, "I love when that happens." She places the can to her lips and very slowly licks the edge and places it to her lips. Then the disclaimer pops on the screen stating, "The manufacture guarantees that the 'Freezesac' will keep ice frozen for over three hours at or below ninety degrees Fahrenheit if left unopened. Opening and closing the 'Freezesac' will shorten it performance level. 'Freezesac' will not make it snow." Most that purchased it were hoping to enter sporting events with it concealed under their coats to save on the high cost of refreshments.

Moving over to the workbench Barry checked his watch to make sure that the "Freezesac" had been out for two hours. "Yep, just a little over two hours. That will give me plenty of time to get just about anywhere I'd like." He pulled the zipper down three-quarters of the way, opening the 'Freezesac.' Lifting the sword out of the sac he felt its weight and a smile of satisfaction crossed his face. Taking a stance like a prizefighter, holding the sword with his right hand on the base and his left holding the blade, half way from the handle to the point, to guide its direction, threw the equivalent of a right uppercut. The force of the punching action drove the sword through the leather, wood strips and the roast in one fluid motion. He was astonished of how easily the ice blade sliced through all three, with the now three inches of exposed tip glistening with the blood carried from the roast. The hardened wood strips were sliced in two just as if a saw blade had passed through them. They had offered hardly any resistance or protection to the roast. The hardened strips of wood had the same hardness as live bone, as a rib to be precise.

Barry stood there looking down at the wonderful site before him; he could see the blade of the ice sword melting even though the roast was only room temperature. "Man will that ever melt quickly at 98.6 degrees." He could hardly contain himself. "Soon, very soon the world would be a better place. One a week should do it. Yep, one a week," He said to the wall, the roast and himself.

Chapter 11

Ryan and Rebecca sat at their kitchen table looking at the black velvet bag that sat on the white cotton crocheted doily, one of the many that had been given to them buy his Aunts. They both had held the bag and tried to determine what it contained. With only the information that it was centuries old, and from the Old Country, that was all for naught, even after the numerous times they tried nothing that they guessed made any sense. Ryan's cell phone began to vibrate causing it to move on the table. He picked it up, flipping it open, pressed the ANS button saying, "Ryan."

"William, Vincent. Do you have the package with you?"

"Yes, I'm here with Rebecca."

"This is good. Do you have a speaker unit?"

Ryan replied "Yes, I just pressed the button turning it on."

"Hello Rebecca, You are well?"

"Yes, Don Bertoline, quite well thank you."

"Good, Good, Please listen very carefully to what I say, and I will not be able to say anything more than what you now hear. There is a Priest by the name of Father Thomas at *The Church of the Cross* in the town of Saint Andrew, New York. This is north of the city 125/135 clicks, sorry 85/90 miles. You must go to him and be in his company the next time I call. This will be two weeks from tomorrow at eleven o-clock P.M. your time. There must be no one else present except you three when I call. There is to be no one told of this. This is of extreme importance. The fate of people very dear to me in our family, depend on your completing this task. Do you understand?"

Ryan started to speak but only got out, "What is this..."

"You must now open the bag. Pull the gold strings apart."

Rebecca slightly tugged on the strings and to her amazement the clasp opened and fell to the table. She pulled the pursed velvet apart and turned the bag opening down and a gold object fell into her hand. It was the size of a bar of soap but only a half-inch thick. A quick flush ran through her body, a moment of warmth that embraced her being. She made a small gasping sound.

"AH, you have it out of the case and you have it in your hand. Yes?"

"Yes," Rebecca replied.

Bill looked at her with a questioning look on his face.

She just smiled back.

"I want you both to inspect it and study it closely. I will tell you how to open it at your meeting with Father Thomas. Please do not attempt to open it or damage it in anyway. The inscriptions on the case, if researched properly will give some answers. Thank you." The phone clicked and read, 'Call Ended.'

The inscriptions were very faint and the case looked like it had been polished and never held. Rebecca looked at the case on all sides then she handed the case to him saying, "Bill, I don't know what dialect that is. I've never seen it before." As he took it from her she watched closely for any reaction. The moment the object touched his hand the same flush of warmth flashed through his body. It startled him for a second, and by his sudden straightening in his seat Rebecca knew that he had experienced the same sensation. Ryan looked at her saying, "I don't know what that was but it was something."

Holding the case at a slight angle he could see the inscriptions that covered both sides of the case. Looking back at Rebecca he shook his head and said, "Well, believe it or not I've had a little exposure to Latin and this looks like an old form of that. That's something we can check on the internet."

Rebecca grinned and replied, "Exposure to Latin, When did this take place?"

Grinning back He said, "Well, Dutch and I were Alter Boys for a few years and ...."

"Altar boys?" Rebecca had a feigned look of shock on her face, trying to not laugh. "You and Dutch?

"Yes, we did it for......"

She couldn't stop herself, she burst into a heart felt laugh and her eyes started to tear.

Ryan couldn't help himself from joining her and they both were laughing so hard that they were crying.

Through the laughter she said, "No wonder the church is in trouble."

The laughter moved up another notch.

Regaining her composure a little she picked up her PDA and punched the letters on the case into it at the Google site and pressed ENTER. It read SEARCHING.......

The screen blinked and the data found displayed one item and one item alone, BODY OF CHRIST.

Ryan looked at the screen and softly said "More than I needed to know right now."

Rebecca looked up from the screen and as she pushed the END button said, "I agree."

Ryan picked up the case and slid it back into the velvet case and pulled the draw strings tight. He picked up the clasp and pulled the strings through it and with just the slightest pressure the clasp sealed itself. He stood up and walked over and placed the bag in the safe and closed it.

Chapter 12

DUTCH LOOKED OUT OF THE window at the waves of people that moved up and down the street as singles, groups and couples, stopping at the different attractions and shows that made up the Las Vegas strip. There were hundreds of people visible, not really anything that should be extraordinary or exciting, but the fact that it was one thirty in the morning made it so. Vegas is truly, the city that never sleeps. He shook his head and thought, "Always activity and people around, finding the man he needed to see, who didn't want to be seen, was going to be a task."

He moved away from the window and sat on the edge of the bed reaching for the phone. Picking up the receiver he dialed the number that his Uncle had given him and counted the rings, hanging up on the seventh ring. He quickly redialed the number and heard a "Yeah" on the fourth ring, as he expected.

"Need to talk to Johnny one-eye." There was a pause and he heard some muffled conversation and glasses clinking together.

A strong voice said, "It's your dime."

"I need to find a lost friend."

"This friend, he is the guy I got a call about from the man in the old country?"

"Yes, I'm the collector."

"Where are you?"

Dutch knew that the man he was talking to by now knew where he was and even knew his room number. "I'm at the Tower in Paris, twenty second floor."

"Okay, I'll be stopping by for a drink in about an hour."

"I'll see you then." Dutch hung up the phone and grinning and thought, "Never asked the room number."

He knew that the man would be there in a half-hour. He walked over to the fully stocked wet bar and dropped a few ice cubes into a glass and lifting the new bottle Gentleman Jack, opened it and poured two fingers of it into the glass and then splashed a bit of vermouth. He glanced at the new bottle of Johnny Walker Gold, grinning thought, "I guess that's Johnny-one-eye's brand."

Walking back to the window he thought about what had brought him to Vegas. Just a little more than twenty-four hours ago he had been sitting in his living room playing with his dogs and feeling very relaxed. Now he was pacing in front of a picture window looking out over what was basically a make believe world of gambling, sex, food, and crime. All of it driven by men's greed and the chance to get something for nothing.

When his phone had rung this past weekend he had no idea that the call would have him on the other side of the country before two days passed. He could still hear the pleading in the voice on the other end of the line. Each word had stung and he could make no other decision than to say yes to the request. The call had been from his Aunt Sophia Scalla, mother of seven of his first cousins. There were six girls, and each one a sensible, kind, intelligent, caring person, and one boy, Freddie, the heart break of his mother's life. His Aunt had explained how her dear Freddie had been forced into a terrible scheme to scam a large sum of money from family members and friends and then disappeared. She had called all of her brothers and they could not find anything out about his whereabouts or health, and everyone else seemed to not care. She believed that something terrible was going to or had happened. He had calmed her down and promised to look into it and let her know as soon as he could about what he learned about Freddie. She had thanked him, and seemed to be much calmer, telling him that he was the only one who ever cared about the family.

After hanging up with her he called his Uncle Sal and inquired about Freddie, the scam and those involved. His Uncle's reaction and exclamation, "Fuck Freddie the Potts," to the questions surprised him. His Uncle then explained the whole story. "Dutch, you know that that boy never had the sense that God gave him. He got mixed up with a few of those skinhead sons - of - a- bitches, and started rolling the drunks and bums in the city and here on the island. After he got his ass kicked a few times he looked for something easier. Well, then he meets this asshole named Kumar- Kaffe and they get the bright idea of selling cheap health insurance from a company that doesn't exist. It seems that a group of Middle Eastern businessmen, friends of Kumar-Kaffe, formed a company and got all of the idiots on the street to sell these policies that weren't worth the paper they were printed on. Well, Freddie sells about a hundred of these useless policies, at six hundred to a thousand bucks each, to the families of city workers, police, fireman and our own family members. This all in about a month and Freddie, being Freddie, splits with the money. Now he has every body looking for him and he is not to be found.

His businessmen friends decided to pressure some of our family for information about his where abouts, and your Uncle Frank and I took objection to that, so we made sure that they got the message to back off. After the loss of a few hands and fingers they got the point. The family is safe but everyone in the family has forgotten Freddie's name. You understand? But this Kumar and his buddies are still hunting him, and I'm sure he will not survive their finding him. The last thing that I could find out about him was that he had taken a bus to Tampa, then poof, he was gone."

Dutch asked a few more questions and the answers he got, or didn't get, told him that there was something much bigger going on. He had thanked his Uncle and wishing him his best hung up.

The second call he made was to his cousin Billy, Detective William H. Ryan of the NYPD, figuring he would have heard anything that had gone through the police department. The call was answered on the first ring.

"Dutch, how are you? Janet?

"Fine, were both well. Rebecca?"

"She's doing great. What's up?"

"Freddie." There was a long pause, "Well, I understand that he's not a very popular guy right now. There are quite a few people looking for him."

"Yes, Quite a few?"

"Well, how about those Yankees?"

"What?"

"Have you talked to our Cousin Danny lately?"

"Danny? I'm talking about Freddie."

"Yes, Danny has a new job, going into business for himself. You should give him a call. Give Janet my best." The phone clicked and Billy was gone.

Dutch remembered standing there just looking at the phone and muttering, "What the hell was that." He waited a few moments and pushed the programmed call button for his Cousin Danny. The phone clicked twice, a buzz, static, and then there were two rings and then he heard his cousin's voice, "Hello Dutch."

"Danny, what was all that?"

"We're on a secure line going through a Federal data scrambler. What's up? Billy just called and said that you were fishing?"

"A federal data scrambler?"

"I'll tell you about it later."

"Okay." There was a moment's pause, "Danny, I'm just looking into what happened to Freddie Scalla. Aunt Sophia called me and said that he disappeared. I asked Billy and he started to say something and then started talking nonsense and hung up."

"Dutch, Tell me what you know?"

He told Danny about all of his calls and how everyone seemed off.

"Dutch, everything you have heard is true. What you and they don't know is that that group of businessmen that Freddie got involved with are being watched by the Department of Homeland Security."

"The Department of Homeland Security?"

"Yes, the scams that they were and still are running are to raise money to fund a very serious mission, they are moving very large amounts of money around the county. They are planning something very big, something that must not be allowed to happen. Dutch, these guys might have a dirty bomb."

"OH Shit, What the hell does Freddie have to do with that?"

"Nothing, we think, but he can finger all of the players. That is why he is gone. We know he got to Tampa but there is nothing after that, nothing."

"Danny, how the hell do you know all of this and just who all is looking for him?"

"Well there are Us, Homeland Security, his businessmen friends and you."

"Who makes up us?

Danny laughed, "I'll tell you when I see you."

"What about using Uncle Sal's resources?"

"No, it was explained to him that that would be a very bad idea to get involved in this in any way. Dutch, it was made very, very clear that this was something to stay away from. It also is a very bad idea for you to go any further with this then this call. For everyone's sake, walk away from this one cousin."

Dutch sat on the arm of his couch staring out of the french doors and said, as he hung up, "Right."

Danny looked at his phone for a few minutes before setting it back in the holder, "Damm it!"

Dutch remembered waiting a few minutes before he switched on his scrambler and pushed the number for his Uncle. The call was answered on the first ring, "Yes, Dutch."

"Uncle, I need to find someone without anyone knowing and there are many important people already looking for him."

"This is family business?"

"A family member is involved in this thing, but in

a small way, but he must be found by me and not the others or he will not be. This thing, Uncle, I believe that it could make New York look like a city in Japan during the war. There are people from your side of the ocean, south of you, involved." There was a long pause.

"Who do you seek?"

"Freddie Scalla.

"Sophia's boy?"

"Yes, she called me and asked me to find him. The last time he was seen was in Tampa, days ago."

"The last I heard was that one of the families was very unhappy with him and trying to find him also. I'll call back, but it will take some time so that it is not noticed. A day, maybe two." There was a click and then a second click.

Dutch had hung up the phone and stood staring out the door seeing nothing.

A day and a half passed before his phone rang twice, stopped, then rang three times. He picked it up saying, "Yes Uncle."

"Call this number when you get to Las Vegas and talk to Johnny One Eye, and see what you can collect. This is all I know or will know." The phone clicked.

The next thing he knew he was on a plane to Vegas for a meeting that never happened with people that don't exist.

Chapter 13

GRAVES WALKED UP TO THE uniform and before he could say anything the officer handed him an evidence bag with the red tape securely placed all around it. The name of the officer was signed on all four sides, front and back, with the time and his badge number. "Found this in the corner of the alley behind the bodega over there. Don't know if it's what you're looking for, but that sure isn't a natural thing growing around here." Graves took the bag and holding up towards the sky replied, "Not unless they grow king size lima beans." The officer laughed, "I never would have thought of that as a description for what's in that bag, now if you said condoms for dogs or some such, I'd agree." They both laughed a little, Graves put the bag in his pocket and then handed the officer a receipt slip that showed the time, date and his badge number which covered the transfer of the evidence to him. "Thanks, I'll be getting this to the lab."

"No problem, sorry it took so long to find it but with the robbery happening almost a week ago we were lucky to find anything at all. Hope it's what you think it is."

Graves waved as he turned back towards his car.

He would get the bag back to the lab and with just a little luck they would find a solid lead that would point them in the right direction.

Chapter 14

---

*B*ARRY REACHED OVER AND LIFTED the pages out of the printer and glancing at them smiled thinking, "The Internet is a wonderful thing, a truly wonderful thing." It had taken him less then two hours to search the data banks of two companies and retrieve everything one could ever need or want to know about six of their employees. Once he had their home addresses, and with a few more searches, probable routes each might take to and from work, their work schedules, and also their shift hours. He looked at the information, a sheet on each person, and tapped the top sheet speaking out loud to no one but the walls said, "This one, tonight. Yes, tonight is the night!" With that he rushed towards the kitchen.

Opening the closet he reached in and took each item out with reverence and placed everything on the table, he then stepped back to take inventory, Freezesac, gloves and light weight long coat. He had stripped the lining out of the coat to make sure that in wouldn't add heat and shorten the life of the Freezesac. The length of the coat offered the perfect cover for the Freezesac it would not be seen hanging over his left shoulder. He had practiced for hours on the move of unzipping and removing the sword in one smooth motion. In just seconds the sword was in his hands and in position for use. He walked over to the counter on the far side of the room and checked the outside temperature. The remote digital display read 67 degrees. He grinned saying softly, "Perfect." He checked his watch and stepped back to the table. He lifted the Freezesac from the table and slung it over his shoulder, adjusting the strap. It hung close to his side just as he had designed it to do. He put on the coat and put the gloves in his pockets, one glove in each. He checked his watch again, smiled and walked towards the door with a purpose.

Stepping out of his door he pushed the button on the remote in his pants pocket locking the door and enabling the security system. He walked briskly towards the entrance to the subway, saying out loud but to himself, "Payback starts today."

Chapter 15

HE KNOCK AT THE DOOR was firm but not aggressive. Dutch walked over to the door and opened it without checking the peep view to see who was there. He knew that it was Johnny-One-Eye. Standing before him was an average looking man dressed in Dockers and golf polo with some local private club's logo just above the pocket.

Dutch extended his hand saying, "Johnny."

The man grinned noticing the glimmer of surprise that flashed across Dutch's face when he opened the door, and took his hand replying "Dutch."

Johnny walked into the room and directly to the wet bar, he lifted the bottle of Johnny Walker Gold and twisted the cap. As he opened the bottle he said, "I guess I don't look the part, we all can't look like hoods. You can close the door, there isn't anyone else coming to this chat."

Dutch closed the door and walked over to the wet bar, standing next to Johnny he reached for his glass and, lifting it, took a sip.

Johnny continued with, "Nice room, like the selection of drinks and really like the view."

"Thanks, someone had the foresight to make sure that the room had all of the comforts, and I realize that we're a long way from Rocky's Men's Club, both in time and distance."

Johnny laughed saying, "Point well taken and well, a person's got to take care of the big man's friends and stay up with the times." Johnny walked over to one of the chairs that surrounded the ornate coffee table that was placed on a raised section of floor that allowed each person seated a spectacular view of the Las Vegas skyline. Taking a seat, softly said, almost to him self, "I love this place."

Dutch moved over and sat at the opposite corner of the table, across from Johnny, leaving both of them an unobstructed view. He took another sip of his drink and waited.

Johnny continued to look out at the skyline that glowed and blinked with a million lights. "The person that you are looking for is with a friend of mine. He is in a safe place that is known to only my friend and me. I really don't know what you want him for, and don't want to. There have been some pretty bad dudes asking around trying to locate him, and they are not the type that once they find someone they bring them home. I have him because of the financial obligations that he owes to family. Up until a short time ago, after I received your call, I did not know the what, or when, something was to be done with him. I now understand that some major events could, or might, occur because of your friend's involvement or ignorance. I really don't want to know the total story unless there is a chance I can directly change the outcome. I have been told that he is yours to have, along with my total support, until I'm told differently." Johnny stood and walked over to the wet bar and carried the bottle of Johnny Walker and Jack Daniel's back to the table. He filled his glass with the Johnny Walker and pushed the bottle of Jack Daniel's towards Dutch. Taking his seat again he looked at Dutch with a firm but quiet look on his face continuing with," I don't want any bullshit, if what I've heard is true and this piece of shit can stop something very bad from happening, it needs to be done. The others that are looking for him will not be a problem as of 8AM tomorrow. Now, what do you want from me."

Dutch leaned just a bit closer, with out even knowing it, and replied, "I need a few things with one of them being the person that you are entertaining."

"Understood."

Both men picked up their glasses and took a sip of their drinks. It was over an hour later that Dutch opened the door and shaking Johnny's hand said, "Thank You."

"No problem, see you." Johnny turned and walked down the hall with not so much as a glance back.

After he closed the door Dutch turned and walked over to the bar, he picked up the pad he had placed there when they had gotten up and started moving towards the door. He tore off the first sheet of paper that he had been making notes on during their meeting and folded it, he push it into his front pocket. The evening was uneventful and he turned in early after a light meal and an hour of TV.

Having spent the better part of the day by the pool, and on the casino floor, entertaining himself Dutch returned to his room, after over hearing the wife of one of the players at the blackjack table he was playing describe a terrible accident that had occurred and was all over the TV news. He pushed the button on the remote and the 42" flat screen came to life in bright and glorious HD TV.

Dutch pushed the recall button on the remote switching back and forth between the two local news stations as the talking heads broadcast the terrible course of events that took the lives of four visitors.

The well endowed red head, with the slightly too tight blouse, was expounding on how the explosion had totally destroyed the single family home. It was determined that the home had been rented to a middle age couple just a few months ago. The owner was an out of state resident that lived in Utah and had never met the renters. It had all been done on the internet with electronic wire transfers for the deposit and rent. The Medical Examiner's first pass at a report stated that there were partial remains of what looked to be from six adults, five men and one woman; the body parts were spread across the yard and the entire fire footprint.

It was being assumed that the four men were visiting the middle aged occupants, if that is what they were in fact, when the explosion occurred; the explosion was so intense that it left nothing but the rear wall of the home intact and a demolished Cadillac SUV in the drive. It was thought that the SUV was rented to one of the victims.

Pushing the button again the second channel's well-endowed blond was standing in the street interviewing a Fire Department Field Captain, with the remains of the destroyed house behind them. There were a dozen men cordoning off what was left of the house with four inch yellow tape. With a perky smile on her face she asked, "Well Captain Delaforo, are there any new developments, or findings, as to the cause of the explosion?"

The Captain, glancing down at her breasts, replied, "Well, our investigators have found Methamphetamine residue and paraphernalia normally used in the manufacturing of the drug Methamphetamine; we have called in the EPA for the clean up. We found about sixty percent of the six resident's bodies, five men and one woman, but it looks like we will not be able to identify them unless we get a hit with their DNA. The parts that were found are burned beyond recognition. I say parts because the blast dismembered each of them into fifteen or twenty pieces each." His grin showed his feelings about the half step backward the young woman took and the look of shock that crossed her face.

"My God, How terrible," She exclaimed.

The Fire Captain replied, "Stuff happens." He turned to walk away but stopped and turned back towards her saying, "Can you use that term on the air?" and walked off leaving her standing there with nothing to say or anyone to say it to.

Dutch pushed the off button, and looked out the window, placing the remote on the top of the TV thinking, "I bet they were the visitors from the City."

He walked over to the bedside table and reached for the phone and picking it up pressed the numbers for the service desk.

"Yes, may I help you?" A woman's voice asked.

"I'll need a cab to take me down town at 6:00 PM, can you have one out front at 5:50?"

"Yes Sir, Is there anything else I can help you with?"

"No, Thank You."

He placed the hand set back into the receiver.

Dutch unfolded the paper that he had jotted notes on during his talk with Johnny-One-Eye the evening before.

Cab to the corner of E100 Fremont Street and 500 Casino Center Blvd. at 6:00 PM, enter Golden Nugget through that door.

6:30PM put three dollar bills into the giant slot machine just inside the door after the maintenance man finishes working on the machine and hit pay out. Put the three large coins in your pocket and step out of the casino entrance.

Enjoy the saxophone playing of Carl "Safe Sax" Ferris.

A woman will come up to you during the show selling paper flowers, ask for and buy the special one for twenty dollars.

After the Viva Vision Show, on the ceiling of Fremont Street, follow the directions enclosed in the heart of the flower.

Dutch shook his head and mumbled to himself, "Just like James Bond,"

He walked over to the bar and pored himself a few fingers of Jack Black over the three ice cubes he had removed from the ever full crystal ice bucket that sat on the bar,

Glancing at his watch he realized that he still had a few hours before he needed to leave and that he had not eaten yet today. He picked up the phone and hit the button for the Concierge; it was picked up on the first ring.

"Yes?"

"Please have a table held for me on the terrace of Mon Ami Gabi Restaurant; I'll be down in twenty minutes."

"Yes Sir, it shall be waiting."

"Thank You."

He washed and changed quickly and was in the elevator in what seemed like moments. He walked to the entrance that led to the terrace of the AB Sin and gave the young lady his room number and she led him to one of the outside tables with a clear view of the Strip and the Bellagio Casino across the street. He orders one of the imported black India Tea's and an assortment of sweet pastries. The restaurant had a selection of imported teas that was by far the largest he had ever seen or knew of anywhere in the country.

Looking across the street, following the music that drifted over him, he watched the waters of the Dancing Fountains of Bellagio begin to dance to Pavarotti. It was a spectacular sight that was as pleasing to the eyes as the ears.

The young lady brought his order and he immersed himself in the wonderful tastes and fragrances, as he watched the sights and sounds passing by that make up every day in Vegas.

The wonderful voice of Celine Dion now came from the Bellagio and he watched the fountain waters dance to the hypnotic sound of her voice. As the show came to an end he finished his second cup of tea and motioned to the waitress for his check, it was almost time for his taxi to arrive. He paid his check and moved out to the main entrance of the casino. One of the valets waved up his cab, and when it stopped opened the rear door for him. Handing the young man a tip he stepped into the cab, a "Have a good evening." followed him into the cab just as the door closed.

"Where to?" The driver asked.

"Corner of Fremont and Casino Center Blvd."

"Nugget?"

"Yes."

The cab pulled out into the ever present congestion of the Boulevard and headed for Old Vegas, the three block strip that was home to the first casinos that made up the Vegas of the fifties and sixties. The part of Fremont Street that is now called the strip is closed to vehicles and covered by the largest TV/Movie screen in the world. 150 feet wide and three blocks long, with a show every half hour starting at7:00 PM each and every night.

The cabbie pointed out all of the construction sites where new Casinos were being built and also pointed out the changes to Caesars. Mentioning that he did not know for sure, but he did believe that Caesars was the largest Casino, by far, in the city. He passed as much info about the city as he could without being pushy in his attempt to increase his tip. He pulled up to the corner of Fremont and Casino with a "Here you are. Hope you have a great time."

Dutch looked at the meter and saw that the trip was fifteen twenty five, he handed the cabbie a twenty and said "Keep the change."

The cabbie grinned and replied, "Thanks Man, here is my card, you need a ride, anytime, call me, I'll be there."

Taking the card Dutch replied, "I'll do that, it will be some time later tonight," He stepped out of the cab and stepped away. He watched the cab disappear around the corner and turned towards the famed Golden Nugget.

He entered the casino and the large slot machine was directly to his left, a man in a blue mechanic's uniform was leaning into the large open panel that was the slot machine's heart. He worked for another five minutes until all the people that were waiting to play the machine drifted off. Turning towards Dutch he said, as he closed the panel's door, "Your lucky day man, no line to play. Good Luck."

Dutch slid the three dollar bills into the money receiver slot and watched the digital numbers record his three plays. He pushed the Pay Out button as instructed and three large silver coins dropped into the payout tray. He pushed in the cover and pulled out the coins, glancing at them he then put them in his pocket and walked out of the casino on to Freemont Street. The coins were larger than a silver dollar and seemed to weigh more, they also had the "Golden Nugget" printed on both sides.

Just a few yards towards the center of the street there was a large crowd of people forming around a musician with a saxophone in his hands. The musician was explaining what he was about to play while the young lady with him spread CD's and literature out on a small table that sat in front of four very large speakers. Just as the musician was finishing his explanation the entire ceiling exploded in a fantastic display of sound and lights announcing the beginning of Carl "SAFE SAX" Ferris' show.

Carl began playing his first song and it was the best Saxophone solo that Dutch had ever heard, here or anywhere else, and it was obvious that the large crowd agreed with him. The people were mesmerized and swayed along with the ebb and flow of the song. Dutch was engrossed as Carl was into playing the third song of the set when he felt a slight tug on his sleeve. He turned to find a very good looking young woman standing very close and holding a small bouquet of flowers in front of her.

She looked up at him, with crystal blue eyes and a smile that would make any dentist proud, and asked, "Would you like to buy a handmade lucky flower?

Dutch smiled and replied, "Why yes I would. Do you have one that you especially like more than the rest, you know, a very special one?"

"Why yes, I do have a very special one, but it costs twenty dollars while the others are only five."

"I'll take the special one, thank you."

She smiled and handed him the only white flower in the bunch, "Here you are."

"Why thank you," Dutch said, as he handed her a twenty dollar bill and took the flower.

The young woman said, "Thanks" as she turned and walked away with not so much as a glance backwards.

Dutch did not show it so much as a second of interest, just folded it with one hand and put it into his vest pocket and listened to the last of Carl "SAFE SAX" Ferris' set. The young lady with Carl had all she could do to keep up with the selling of the CD's. Dutch walked over and shook Carl's hand and thanked him for a great show and then purchased copy of Carl's latest CD.

As Dutch walked toward Casino Center Blvd, he leaned against the pole that held the "walk – don't walk sign" as it flashed a red hand signaling, "Don't Walk." He pulled the paper flower out of his pocket and slowly unfolded it. While watching the show he had pulled it apart and unfolded it while it was still in his pocket. On the inside of the paper was a note that while the paper was folded, and crimped into a flower looked like seeds in the base of the petals.

The note read, cross Casino Center and continue to the next block on the left, 3rd Street. Go left and go to Hogs and Heifers Saloon; it will be on your left. Go in and order a Jack on the Rocks and ask for 'Red', when 'Red' and the Jack arrive, pay for the drink with the three Coins from the Nugget.

As he stood there waiting for the street light to change the ceiling flashed to life and a burst of color shot from one end of the screen to the other, traveling all three blocks. Then a space ship appeared and the dialog explained that the earth was under attack from outer space beings. Our F-15 jets appeared and the battle for earth spread across the screen speeding from one end to the other in seconds, with giant aliens walking across the ceiling, the war took about eight minutes of great color displays, action and sound. Thank the Lord, the earth was saved! The crowd of hundreds clapped and cheered.

Dutch thought about how the show was the best set up ever for a pick pocket, hundreds of people standing around looking up and not giving a nudge or bump any thought. "Dam, I've got to stop thinking like that," he thought to himself with a grin. The light was favorable so he started across the street and after a few minute's walk stood in front of the Hog's and Heifer's Saloon. There were twenty or so bikes parked in front, mostly Custom Harley's. Of all of the posters and signs pasted or hung on the outside of the place the one that was most prominent read, **"No wearing of colors allowed!"**

"Damn smart rule," he thought. He didn't need to walk into a feud between two biker gangs.

Chapter 16

GRAVES PULLED THE PAGES OF the DNA report out of his printer glancing at them as he walked towards Ryan's office. He tapped the doorframe as he entered, seeing Ryan on the phone he stopped short. Ryan looked his way and waved him to a seat.

"Yes Sir, I believe we are very close to a breakthrough on that case." He held the phone a little further from his ear. "Yes Sir, you will be the first to know. Thank You, Good bye." He pushed the End button and placed the phone on the desk. Looking at Graves said, "The Chief of D's is getting a lot of heat from the local business' owners about the robberies. Seven robberies in six weeks, and the media is beating us up pretty good. I hope you have some good news."

Graves shook his head replying, "Not so good Lou, they couldn't get a useable print off of the spray skin we found. The only good news is we do have a DNA signature. I ran it through the data base and came up empty, but if we can find the guy the DNA will lock up the case."

"Well, I guess that's something. By any chance did they do a profile on the DNA?"

"Yea, I asked them to do a work up and it came back; Complexion - Light, Ancestry - Caucasian/Oriental."

"Well that narrows it down to about a million people just south of Twenty-Third Street. It's been three days since the last robbery and the only day of the week this guy hasn't worked is on a Thursday. Today is Tuesday, It's my bet that he will be out and about this Thursday night, and it's well known that the construction crews building the new sky scraper all get paid cash on Friday. The check cashing houses are fronting the money to the companies with crews on that site, so they don't have to carry all that cash very far, those guys still get paid cash on site each Friday. I know that it's only a hunch, but my best guess is that his next job will be this Thursday."

"Well, your guess is better than most facts, Lou, should I have a splash of uniforms or all undercover?"

"Undercover, I'll talk to the Uniform Captain down stairs and see if he'll give us a squad that can play Detective for a few nights if needed. We'll try it Thursday and if nothing happens we'll try again Friday. Most of the robberies have been in an eight-block area, and his way in has been off of an alley each time. Run a data scan for all of the financial and check cashing storefronts in that area, we want the blocks that don't have a bank on them. I'm pretty sure this guy knows about the fish eye cameras that the banks have installed to cover the exterior entrances and exits"

"Got it, by the way I did check the videos of all of the banks, within a block of each of the other hits. They all came up empty." Graves stood and headed for the door.

"On your way ask Malone to come see me."

"You got it, Lou"

Ryan picked up his phone and pushed the code for the Captain. He was not surprised when the call was answered with, "William, how can I help?" The Uniform Captain was a great guy in every respect. He was from the old school and Ryan had never heard him use anything but a proper name or full rank when addressing any fellow officer. If you got the full rank and name that meant that you were held on a totally business level and no more.

"Cap, if it is possible, I would like to use one of your squads for an undercover operation Thursday and maybe Friday night. I will be something like 4PM to Midnight."

"I don't for see a problem with that, I'll check with the Squad Sergeant. Is this for the "Rash of Robberies" that the media is howling about?

"You got it, the media, and the Chief, are up in arms. Can you have the Squad Sergeant contact Graves? He will be leading it up."

"It will be done this shift and if any of the Media happens to get in the way they can spend a few nights in my holding cell."

"Thank you."

"Anytime I can help, William." The phone went dead.

Ryan put the phone down and grinned, thinking about the last statement, "I'm sure glad he's on my side."

Chapter 17

*D*UTCH *OPENED THE DOOR AND* stepped into the Hog's and Heifer's Saloon, it took a moment for his eyes to adjust to the change in lighting. He was facing a forty to forty five foot bar that ran away from the entrance door. There were about twenty five or so men and women sitting and standing at it. There was a young woman behind the bar with a megaphone blaring out an obscenity towards one of the men standing by a machine with a punching bag on it. There was a CD player on the far wall and a woman was sitting in front of it with a play selection book on her lap. He noticed that there were no tables and chairs to be found anywhere, but at the far end of the building.

He walked up to the closest end of the bar and took a seat; he was watched by most of the men and all of the women. The girl behind the bar stepped over and with a big smile asked, "What the fuck can I get you?"

Without missing a beat, and showing no reaction to the young woman's statement, Dutch replied, "A Jack on the Rocks, and send 'Red' over."

She grinned replying, "Done!" She turned and

walked away. She put ice in a glass and filled it with "Jack." She picked up the megaphone and announced, "The man wants a "Jack" on the Rocks and to see 'Red.'

The woman at the CD player got up and walked towards the rear of the building and the opening to the back of the bar, she turned and walked towards the front picking up Dutch's drink on the way. She stopped in front of Dutch and placed the drink down saying, "That's your "Jack" and I'm 'Red' so what's next?" The smile on her face lit up everything within six feet it seemed.

Dutch placed the three coins from the Golden Nugget on the bar and waited. 'Red' picked up the coins and smiling said, "Pick up your drink and follow me Dutch." With that she turned and walked back the way she had come. The eyes of every man at the bar watched her intently, slowly turning their heads to follow her every movement and there were many things moving.

Dutch got his drink and followed her, step for step, down the bar; she came around the end of the bar and stepped up on a platform that held two red vinyl couches that looked like they came from a fifty's soda shop. The walls were curved to give the appearance that the couches were in a sort of cove. 'Red' sat in the one facing the bar and motioned for Dutch to sit next to her.

Dutch sat next to 'Red' and knew that not many were offered the opportunity to do so from the reaction of the other patrons.

'Red' stood about five feet five inches and weighed about one hundred and eight pounds, with zero body fat. He guessed she had about a thirty eight inch bust, a twenty two inch waist and thirty inch hips. Shoulder length red hair, pouty lips, sparkling eyes and a smile that just did not quit, she looked like a prefect prettier version of one the star investigators of one of the most popular Vegas Crime/Police shows on TV. She wore jeans that seemed to be painted on, boots with three inch heels, and a white stiff leather halter top that tied in the front with leather ties and was held in place by leather strings that crisscrossed from front to back on each side of her neck. Everything was where it was suppose to be and in the correct quantities, she was stunning to say the very least.

'Red' rolled the Golden Nugget Coins in her hand as she sat looking at him, "Well, you're a lot more than I expected. Expected a very over weight and over the hill NY Cop with a note pad in one hand and a bullshit story in the other."

"Sorry I disappointed you."

'Red' laughed a genuine laugh replying, "I'm not!"

Dutch took a sip of his drink and waited for her to continue.

She slipped two of the coins into her front pocket and to his amazement twisted the remaining coin with her finger tips and it came apart allowing a slip of paper to fall out. "This is part of what I am to give you. There is a similar paper in each of the other coins with more of the information you are looking for. Do you mind if we talk bit before we get into those?"

"Not at all, anything special you want to talk about?"

She grinned asking, "Married?"

"Yep."

"Darn, well, how about having dinner anyway?"

"Love to, let me make a few calls. What time is good?"

"I'm out of here at eight, live ten minutes from here, ten or so to clean up a bit, eight thirtyish okay?"

"That works for me. Do you have a car or is a taxi alright?"

"Taxi works for me." She smiled and handed him the paper, standing said,"I've got to work a bit, stay here and do what you need to. No one will bother you."

"Be my pleasure."

'Red' leaned down and brushed his lips with hers and turning to walk away said with a laugh, "All the good ones are always taken."

Dutch watched her walk away and when she was behind the bar turned to the paper she had given him. It was the beginning of step by step instructions to getting Freddie back in one piece. He thought it was all a little James Bondish but he also realized that if anything went wrong thousands might be lost. No one wanted that on them. He picked up his phone and called his hotel and asked for the Concierge's desk. The Concierge listened to his request for help in getting dinner reservations at Michael Mina's Restaurant in Bellagio's at eight forty five.

He assured Dutch that a table would be waiting for him where ever he and his guest got there. Dutch thanked him and hung up. Next he called the cabbie that had brought him to Fremont Street, the cabbie answered on the second ring, "Always ready cab, Robert speaking."

"Robert, Dutch, I need you to pick me up at the Hog's and Heifer's Saloon on third street at eight, we'll have a stop in between but we'll end up at Michael Mina's in Bellagio's."

"You got it, I'll be out front."

"Thanks." Dutch put his phone away and watched as 'Red' danced her way, on top of the bar, from one end to the other. She saw him watching and winked as she high stepped between two glasses that sat in the middle of the bar.

Chapter 18

BARRY MOVED ACROSS THE STREET, with a glance to his right and left, feeling as if he were gliding. This was the time, the time to start squaring things for the everyday guy, the workhorse of the economy, and the leader of what was right. Yes, all of this starts today; his head was almost spinning with the feeling of goodness. "Today things will start to be as they should be," he thought as he reached the top step leading down to the platform. He saw everyone on the platform but saw no one, four stops north, two blocks east and again down to the waiting subway platform. That is where he will step into the world of right. He stepped onto the train and fought to keep the grin off of his face.

He watched each person that entered with a blank look of boredom showing on his face. The car jerked forward with a sudden lurch and the trip he had waited for, for the past year had begun. The time passed almost with no sensation, second stop, third stop, forth stop. Doors open, stand and walk across the platform, up the stairs and on to the street. Check traffic, cross street, walk two blocks, down stairs, take seat on platform, wait.

From the information learned from the internet and the work schedules that he studied so carefully Barry knew that his prey would be there and on time. It all was happening as if a dream, a wonderful dream. He glanced up at the two video cameras that were to keep the platform under surveillance and smiled seeing both still dangling from the wires facing down towards the floor.

He watched the train pull into the station, and screech to a halt, his anticipation was growing to a point that he almost could not stand it. When the train came to a complete stop the doors opened and his prey stepped through the doors. He stepped out on to the platform, standing tall with his deep blue security coat pressed and tailored to display his brute form, the form of a by the hour security officer that was nothing but a make believe cop.

Barry glanced around the platform and was pleased to see that it was deserted. "Just you and me big boy," he thought.

The security officer started walking towards the steps that led up to the street, he glanced at the poorly dressed man with a slouched hat sitting on one of the benches and disregarded him like so much trash. As he passed the man on the bench he kicked at the man's shoe with a laugh, he missed which made him laugh louder. He was about two feet past the man when the man on the bench stood and made the motion like he was throwing an upper cut. There was no sound except for the sound of the security guard folding into a heap on the platform floor.

The ice sword had cut through the rear of the man's

ribcage, and passed right through his heart, he was dead before he hit the floor.

Barry looked down at the mass of blue that lay before him and watched the puddle of bright crimson red form around it. "One for the good guys, many more to come," Barry thought as he hurried to, and up the steps to the street. He reversed his travel and in what seemed to be moments, but was still forty minutes, he was walking across the street to his home. His face hurt from keeping the grin from showing, he had done it and it all went just as planned, just as planned and it was so easy.

Chapter 19

---

*M*ALONE PUSHED THE SEND BUTTON, her report and her recommendations were on their way to the Borough Commander on the island. She had been working with him on the restructuring of his tactical squad's procedures for handling hostage and family crisis situations. She picked up a hard copy of the data and headed for Ryan's office. She would also forward a copy of the sent e-mail and the attachment that she sent, from her SENT file, to him so it could be archived in his back up files.

She enjoyed the times that she worked with other Precincts, and different Departments, even though she knew some of them considered her strange due to her special ability. Her ability was one of the best known secrets in law enforcement and she knew that it was only Ryan's clout that kept them from abusing her time and efforts. She was the reason that many of the high profile cases, local-state-and federal, across the county had been broken. What she learned through her ability could not be directly used in court but helped the right questions to be asked and areas to be searched.

When she was asked to help on a case it was extremely important that nothing she learned was directly introduced as evidence. If it was, it would be found to be unconstitutional and information recovered without a warrant. The case would be lost, every time. These were the only reasons that she was not overwhelmed with demands on her time. That and Ryan, of course.

Walking into Ryan's office a shutter ran through her body and she realized something, something was missing, the buzz that she lived with every waking hour suddenly stopped and was not there. She had had been working on the report and subsequent e-mail since seven this morning and really hadn't noticed the reduction of the white noise, that was ever present in her head. She grabbed for the chair and just barely made it into the seat. Tears seemed to explode from her eyes and a deep sigh escaped her lips.

Ryan jumped from his chair and was next to her in a moment, "Malone, what's wrong?

She continued to sob.

Ryan pushed the buttons on his phone and yelled, "Get the paramedics up here, Now!"

Malone seemed to gain some composure and touching his hand shook her head saying, "No, No, call them off. Just give me a moment, please."

By this time there were six people trying to get through Ryan's door at the same time. At least half of them had guns drawn.

Ryan stood and waved his hand saying, "It's okay, it's okay, everybody calm down. I've got it under control. Please go back to your work." Moving some of them toward the door continued with, "Okay, everybody, back to what you were doing. Thank you. Graves, call off the Medics."

Looking at Malone, and then Ryan, replied, "Got it Lou." He ushered the last person out the door and closed it on his way out.

Ryan stepped next to the chair Malone was still sitting in and knelt beside it saying, "You okay?"

Malone had a tissue in her hand and was dabbing her eyes. She looked at him and said, "Ryan, the noise is gone."

"The noise, what noise?"

"The slight buzzing of voices that has been going on in my head 24/7, ever since I can remember, it's just gone."

Ryan didn't know what to say but stammered, "Is, is that good?"

Malone looked at him and replied, "I don't know, I really don't know."

Ryan reached over and grabbed the other chair and pulled it over. He sat in the chair next to her, and he thought, "I can't begin to know what she must be going through,"

Malone looked up at him with a startled look on her face and said, "I just heard everything you just thought and that only. My God, I can pick who and when I want to read. The only way I can describe it is, it's like,,,, it's like selecting a song on an album. Everything before was always like hearing a song playing just a little louder than the one playing in the next room." She started to wipe the tears away that started to run freely down her cheek again. "My God, I've never ever heard quite before. It's wonderful."

Ryan reached over and took her hand and just sat there in silence, Malone had a contented smile on her face. They sat there for about ten minutes before Malone looked at Ryan saying, "Sorry, It overwhelmed me, I still can't believe it. You wanted to see me about something?"

Ryan stood and walked around his desk, back to his chair. He grinned saying, "Well, I was going to ask you how things were going. You've looked preoccupied lately but I guess this explains that."

"Not really, I guess I have been walking around sort of in a daze. For a while now every time I walked from the subway, either from or going to home or work, it felt like there were a million tiny bugs crawling around in and on my head. That and the seemingly louder white noise in my head was just about to drive me crazy. This morning I came in a little earlier and when I left the subway stairs down the street the bugs went away. It was sudden, you know? Like when you are walking in a teeming rain and you walk under a walkway canopy."

Ryan shook his head in acknowledgement and asked, "Any idea what was causing the bugs?"

"No, I was real careful about being tailed and never noticed any one just watching me. I tried to read a bunch of people but never came up with anything. The scan alarm that I made second nature never went off with anything but the normal stuff."

"Scan Alarm?"

She smiled and replied, "I would get a instant read if someone was thinking about me. Like if I'm walking down the street and a guy walking the opposite way sees me and thinks something. Like 'nice legs' and such."

Ryan shook his head and replied, "How did you stay sane?"

Malone grinned as she stood and reached over put her hand on his saying, "I have some good friends that have always cared about me and thought good thoughts."

"I don't know anything about how you could, and can, do what you do but I'd keep and eye open. I don't think stuff like this just happens."

"You bet." Malone stood and continued, "If its okay with you Boss, I would like to go home and sit in silence for a few hours with my own thoughts for once."

Ryan stood and replied, "Of course, call and let me know that you got home without anything happening. You can let me know when you are coming back in then."

Malone turned and as she walked out of the room turned and said, "Thank you Lou. I'll call, but I'll see you in the morning."

Chapter 20

DUTCH FINISHED HIS SECOND "JACK" and placed the glass on the small table that sat next to the sofa as he looked up over the punching machine at the clock. "Seven fifty, about time to move on," he thought. Just as if it were magic 'Red' came around the corner from the back of the bar with a smile on her face and a "Lets blow this place on her lips. He stood and gave her an affirmative nod as he stepped off the platform and towards the door.

'Red' grabbed his hand and gave it a squeeze saying,"Just have to break their hearts," as they walked to the front door. Every eye in the place was on them as they exited the saloon, 'Red' called back to Sadie as she stepped through the door, "Make sure I've got something to come back to in the morning."

Letting the door to the Hogs and Heifers swing closed behind him Dutch almost broke out in a laugh as he gave her hand a squeezes replying, "Always the last word."

She squeezed back and said, "most times."

Dutch saw Robert standing at the rear door of his

cab holding the door open. 'Red' stepped into the cab saying, "Thank you Robert."

Dutch steeped into the cab and glancing back and forth from 'Red' to Robert said, "I guess it's safe to guess that you know each other."

'Red' laughed replying, "Drives me home four or five nights a week. Not worth having a car, and all the associated cost and hassle, if you work anywhere on the strip. Robert we'll be going to my place first."

Starting the cab and pulling away from the curb Robert replied, "On the way."

They pulled in front of a two story stucco home after just a seven or eight minute drive. Robert got out and opened the rear door. 'Red' stepped out saying, "Dutch, come in for a few moments. Robert will wait for us, Right Robert?"

"You bet yours for the night if needed."

'Red' just smiled as she walked up the sidewalk to the front doors to the home. She reached into her pocket and pulled out a card which she slid into the card reader that was mounted next to the door knob. The door popped open about a half inch and she grabbed the door knob and pulled it open the rest of the way. Just before entering she reached in and a ceiling light came on, she looked at Dutch and said, "Okay to go in now."

As they stepped into the house Dutch glanced to his left and saw what he had suspected was there, a fingerprint reader. Had they entered directly after the door popped ajar without 'Red' hitting the reader the security system would have sounded a silent alarm and the police would have been there in moments. "That is pretty slick for a waitress's house."

'Red' turned and grinned, "Yep. Have a seat; I'll be

out in a few moments. Where are we eating dinner? She asked as she disappeared out of sight around a corner.

"Michael Mina's Restaurant," I thought a little Italian would be nice after a hard few hours of trying to keep up with you."

"Sounds great, I love there seafood antipasti and French Fried Lobster Tail with a side of linguini in garlic, oregano and olive oil."

"That does sound great, I can truly say I've never had French Fried Lobster Tail."

Stepping back into the room 'Red' looking at him coyly, replied, "Don't tell me you have never ever had fried tail before."

Dutch turned towards her voice to respond and just stopped. 'Red' had changed into a pair of elegant silk forest green slacks, that clung in all the correct places, power green blouse, with a clam shell neckline, gold open toed two inch heels and also a white scarf strung loose enough around her neck, to border the blouse's neck line, allowing the single gold broach that hung around her neck to take center stage, just above the crest of the rise of her breasts. Her red hair looked like soft flames licking across the white scarf. The contrast of colors was fantastic and all of the pieces fit perfectly. All Dutch said as he stood was, "Wow!"

'Red' smiled and replied, "Well that was well worth it." She moved towards the front door looking back at Dutch saying, "Coming?"

Chapter 21

GRAVES STOOD IN FRONT OF the twenty four uniforms and outlined the operation that they would be taking part of that evening. He pointed to the map, on the pull down screen, and pointed to the four check cashing houses that they would be keeping under surveillance. There would be four teams of six, with the six broken into three sub teams of two. One across the street and in front of the cash house under surveillance, one a few doors left or right depending on which way gave a clear view of the front door, and one in the building under surveillance, on the second or third floor if there was one.

He pointed to the street maps and went over the access points to each cash house and pointed out the places each sub team would be stationed for the duration of the stakeout. There were a few questions that he replied to and he gave each team their call name and explained that no more than three from each team, one from each sub team, was to respond to a call for assistance unless it was a "officer down" call. He knew that some of what he was going over was pretty basic but more than half of these men had never worked plainclothes before and he did not need anyone attempting to be "Super Cop."

Ryan walked into the room and it went silent at once. He looked at each man and nodded to the ones he recognized. "Tonight we hope to put an end to the rash of burglaries that has been terrorizing Chinatown and the surrounding area. Our perp is smart and does his homework, keep out of sight if you are to be and relaxed if you are positioned on the street. If you look like you're looking for someone you will be made in a skinny minute. If something comes down do just what you were told, don't be a hero, hero's die young. Use your radios, but use then with care. I will be in an unmarked unit from one of the vice squads uptown. If you see the perp enter a site, wait till he in before you make the radio call. He has been so successful with his past jobs he will not be in a rush, we don't need to be either. There has not been any injuries related to this case as of yet. Let's try and keep it that way, any questions?"

There was no response, just a lot of eager faces. "Okay, do what LT. Graves has instructed you to do and maybe we'll catch us one tonight, and all go home with a story to tell." He turned and walked out of the squad room giving Graves a wink as he left.

He walked back to his office and stood looking out the window, his phone vibrated on his belt. He pulled it out of the holder, and he grinned seeing "Slim" on the display. He flipped it open and pressed the talk button saying, "Hello good looking."

"That will get you everything, Hello back. Two things, I know that you will be late tonight but I've got Doctor Stephens' class, with a Lab after it, at the

Medical University tonight and it will not be over till somewhere around eleven thirty or twelve. I was thinking that if you're done by then, give me a call, and we can meet for a bite to eat. Does that sound okay to you?"

"Sure does, I'll call whenever we get done, one way or the other, and the second thing?"

"Oh, I got one in this afternoon that I think you need to take a look at. Very strange case, the Detective that came in for the autopsy was totally confused, asked me to ask you to take a look if you could. His name was Cirrilo and said he knew you."

"Cirrilo, sure he worked a case for me and used to date Malone a while ago. I'll set some time aside tomorrow and drop over to take a look. Hey, let's do lunch, Vinny's is on me, I'll stop by at eleven. I'll call later when I can, Love You."

"Sounds great, Love you too."

The phone displayed 'Call Completed.'

Ryan turned to sit at his desk just as Graves walked into the room.

Ryan waved him into the chair across from the desk as he sat down.

"Well Lou, Those guys are pumped. I sure hope that they haven't seen any Bruce Willis movies lately. We sure don't need any of them playing shoot'em up on the streets at nine o'clock at night.

"That we don't need at any time of the day or night. If they stay cool we might get lucky and catch this guy, if he shows."

"All we can do is hope; I'm going to be a stumbling drunk, stumbling around in a six square block area. I might get one pass through the whole thing before I have to whole up somewhere. I just have to see how it goes."

"That sound good, I'll stay stationary most of the time unless we get some radio chatter. I'll start in the middle of the stakeouts and move out counter clockwise using the one way streets. Graves, I've been thinking about this, keep your eyes out for any kind of deliver or service vehicles. This guy disappears too fast for my liking. Maybe he hasn't been seen because he's one of the invisible people of New York."

"Got it, that's been bothering me also, Lou."

They both knew that the invisible people of New York were the thousands of delivery and service people that moved in and out of buildings each and every day, without so much as a glance by the occupants of those buildings. No one sees them, or remembers them, not what they look like, sound like, nothing.

Graves walked back into the squad room and looking at the officers seated there said, "Its time, leave in your assigned team groups, with a few moments between groups. We don't want to look like the Third Army storming the beaches leaving the house. Give me a radio check once you are in position, good luck and most of all, stay alert."

The men stood and the first team headed for the door.

It took almost an hour for all of the men to get out and in position, the radio check was called in by each sub team and the waiting began.

Ryan pulled his car into an alley and followed it until he was stopped just before the side walk across the street from the largest check cashing house under surveillance that night. He looked into the rearview mirror and asked the electronic surveillance officer in the rear seat if he had any readings from the check cashing house.

"No Sir, all dark and no heat sources found."

The officer had scanned the house with a high intensity infra red heat scanner.

It was on the street that the four check cashing houses were holding almost three quarters of a million dollars to cover the payroll for the construction crews two blocks away. They were building a new one hundred and fifty floor sky scraper and were working five twelve's. Forty hours at their regular hourly rate and twenty hours at double time. A construction workers dream job that came around once every few years. This building would replace the Twin Towers as the king of the New York City skyline.

The darkness of the night was added to as a slight drizzle started to fall. This was going to be one hell of a night for a stakeout. The time passed slowly and there was little if any radio chatter, they had taken his words to heart.

Graves slowly moved down the street, moving with one hand on whatever wall or window he was next to, and a brown paper bag with a bottle in it, in the other. He would stop every few steps and take a hit off of the bottle. He had gone about three blocks and was sitting on the bottom step of a six story walk up when a mini-van turned the corner. The driver was going very slow and gave Graves a long look over, drove past, and then pulled to the curb past an alley on the other side of the street. The driver then backed up into the alley, the alley was half way up the street from the steps Graves was sitting on, to the corner. The alley ran back to the adjoining block, and one of the check cashing houses was one store down from the alleys mouth at that end. The rear exit path of the check cashing house left the rear of the building, and made a left turn onto a walkway to the alley proper.

Graves rose and continued his stumbling, stopping, drinking trip down the street, without so much as a glance towards the alley and the min-van. Graves had not seen a light come on and go off that might have signaled the door of the van being opened, but he was sure that the perp was smart enough to do two things. Disconnect the door light switch and exit the min-van from the rear. With the van backed into the ally at a slight angle, the perp was assured of stopping anyone from getting past it unless they climbed over it. He was sure that if that was done that would sound an alarm of some sort.

The three sub teams, of two officers, watching this check cashing house, were stationed as planned. One in the building across the street with a view of the alley and front of the building, one on the roof across the street, due to the fact that there had been no access to the floors above the Cash house, and one in a junk car half a block down, and across, the street. He had hoped that one of the sub teams across the street would report some activity in the alley, but the perp must have concealed himself somehow. That of course is, if this person is the perp, and not some night worker that lived in the area or any other damn thing that could be.

Having made it to the corner, and falling around it, away from the side of the street the alley was on, Graves pushed the call button on his radio and said, "Bravo Team Two?"

"Bravo Two."

"Leader Two- Any activity or movement in your area of responsibility?"

"None."

"Bravo Team Three"

"Bravo Three."

"Leader Two- Any activity or movement in your area of responsibility?"

"None."

"Bravo Team Three."

"Bravo Three."

"Leader Two- Any activity or movement in your area of responsibility?"

"None."

"Ten Four, Leader Two out."

Graves switched bands and pushed the button again saying, "Leader one, Leader Two, Possible action cash house four. If so entry by way of rear door, alley blocked and possible alarmed on back side, access not available."

Ryan responded, "Leader Two, any access via adjoining buildings?"

Graves laid himself out on the sidewalk on his back and looked at the buildings on each side of the alley across the street. He reached and placed his hand on his head and moaned loudly. He rolled slowly to his right and out of sight of anyone that might be watching from the alley. "Building on the left is a five story walk up, should be able to get through the first floor hallway to a rear doorway. Need to know if the perp is in the check cashing house building. I can't take a chance showing myself again if he is not."

"Okay, I'm going to do a slow drive by and hit the place with an infra red scan, I'll only get one pass and it will be quick. If I get a reading I'll turn left and stop on the corner closest to your position."

The electronic surveillance officer nodded his affirmation to Ryan's statements.

Ryan continued, "We can both go in through the walk up. If it's a go, you need to get all of our acting detectives out there to stand down unless specifically called in."

"Got it."

Graves switched bands again and pressing the send button said, "Leader Two to all teams, stand down, stand down unless specifically called for action, all arms locked 'Safe,' Copy?" Graves waited for the responses, each team called in their affirmative response." He pushed the button again saying, "Bravo team, stand down, but be ready to respond to my location ASAP if called." He again hoped that he did not have any cowboys out there.

Ryan started the car and pulled out of the alley turning left, he had to make a full circle of four turns to make sure he passed the suspect house from the correct direction. The officer in the rear of the car pointed the scan gun at the check cashing house as soon as they turned onto the block but knew that any chance of a reading would only come from when they were directly in front of the building. Ryan knew that he could not pass to slowly for if the perp was glancing out the window and took notice of the car, he would be gone and Graves would be in danger. As they passed the alley Ryan said, "Get ready, one more doorway."

"We have a slight reading, could be a dog or someone with a cool suit on. Sorry Lou that's the best I could get." The officer in the rear seat reported once they had passed the store front.

Ryan pulled around the corner and hit the radio, "Leader Two, cross and meet." With that he opened the car door saying, "Stay here, and watch that corner. If a min-van comes screaming out of there, chase him down."

Ryan knew that the min-van would most likely go the other way if it got to that, but it was one way to ensure the officer staying with the car. There was nothing like the possibility of a high speed car chase to keep someone's interest, and in the driver's seat.

He met Graves just as he was crossing the street and removing the oversized trench coat he had been wearing. They hurried to the front door of the walk up and were not surprised when they found the door unlocked. They quickly moved through the first floor of the building and found the read door that they expected to find. It too was unlocked.

Ryan reached up and unscrewed the bulb in the hallway light and slowly opened the rear door. Graves moved through the door first and then Ryan, they moved down the path away from the building, and came to the path that dissected the walkway between the two rows of buildings. Left would take them to the check cashing house and right to the alley. They moved to their left and stopped at the second path from the alley on the far side of the walkway.

"I'll kick in the door and you go in low and announce, I'll follow high, hopefully we'll get a jump on him and no one will get hurt. We'll be surprising the perp or have a pissed off guard dog all over our asses." Ryan was grinning as he started up the path.

Graves said lowly, "Lord, I hate guard dogs."

As soon as they reached the door Ryan stepped into a kick at the door, it landed right next to the lock, the door frame gave way and the door swung open with a loud crash. Graves was into his rolling entrance and Ryan was charging in, trying to stay sideways to the room to present a smaller target. He heard Graves yell, "Police, freeze. Put your hands up!"

The next thing Ryan knew he was going down tangled up with the perp, who had tried to run over Graves and out the open door, running directly into Ryan as he charged in. Ryan reached and grabbed whatever he could grab and rolled his weight against it.

The next thing he knew Graves was standing over him saying, "Let go Lou, Let go!"

Ryan pushed himself up and stood there looking at Graves with the perp with hands behind his back and heard the sound of cuffs snap into place. The perp was shorter then Graves and still had a mask on. Ryan reached over and pulled the mask off and was surprised to find the face that looked like it belonged to a child looking at him. Ryan did not believe that the perp could be twenty, maybe eighteen, maybe and look to weigh in at 90 pounds. The perp was dressed just like he had been in tapes of the other robberies and Ryan could see the sheen on his hands from the spray gloves.

Graves hit the button on the radio and said. "Bravo Team meet me in the mouth of the alley at your location, all other units stand down, perp is in custody, stand down. All teams return to the house for debriefing. Be sure to fill out your' Fives' first thing."

A stream of "Ten four's and a few' Damn It's' in the back ground" came back.

Graves laughed to himself, he knew that a few of the uniforms were disappointed that they had not seen any action. He made a note to himself to make sure that a personal letter of 'Thank You' went to each of the uniforms for their professionalism during the operation so it would become part of their permanent job file.

Chapter 22

DUTCH READ THE THREE NOTES he had gotten from 'Red' one last time before he put a match to them and dropped the remains in the toilet, flushing them. He walked back out into the main room and slipped his vest on, snapping the bottom button, this kept the vest closed just enough so that should he be wearing a shoulder holster, and gun, it would not show. He picked up the wireless room phone and hit the button for the front desk. It rang twice and he heard, "May I help you?"

"Please have my car brought around."

"Yes sir, it will be at the main entrance."

"Thank you." Dutch pushed the 'End' button and placed the phone on the table with its end touching the middle of the binding of the book that sat in the middle of it. He gave the room a long look, taking note of the position of each item. Satisfied that he could note any change, he opened the door and placed the "Do not disturb" sign on the outside handle and walked towards the bank of elevators.

As the elevator made its way down to the main floor

he had a great view of the Casino floor, it was an ever evolving mass of people and color. When the doors opened he stepped out and moved just to the right side of the doors. He took his wallet out of his pocket and appeared to be checking a piece of white note paper that he took from it. He spent about a moment glancing at the paper and then the far wall as if he was deciding something. Putting the wallet back he turned and proceeded to the main entrance. He walked a bit slower than he normally would have and he did not see any movement, or lack of, that caused suspicion. When he stepped out on to the plaza one of the doormen waved at him and stepping towards a Red Equinox said, "I've got the door for you sir."

Dutch moved toward the open door and getting in passed a ten-dollar bill to the man. The man put up his hand saying, "No need, all has been taken care of. Be sure to use you're seatbelts and the GPS system. There are requested items located in the center console." With that said he closed the door and moved to the next vehicle in line.

Dutch placed the SUV in drive and reached up and pushed the GPS' go button, a pleasant female voice, with the hint of an English accent, said, "Proceed fifty feet and turn right, proceed twenty seven point six miles to a Y in the road. Please take the left fork, US 62 West."

Pulling forward to the entrance to the main road, and glancing left, pulled out into the light traffic that flowed unobstructed out of the city as far as the eye could see. Once out of the main strip area he pulled over into an egress that was built for some future complex. Lifting the console lid he found just what he expected. There was a S&W compact forty-five caliber, semi automatic in a smooth grained shoulder holster and four extra clips. He took the pistol out of the holster and removed the clip, pulling back the slide he was not surprised to see a round in the chamber. The pistol was a Smith and Weston, Police Detective model, with black posit-a-grip inlaid grips. He slipped off the vest and put on the shoulder holster and the vest and clipped the spare clip case on the left side of his belt. There was a small tri pocket wallet that held a driver's license and weapons concealed carry permit under the same name that the rental papers for the SUV displayed.

Satisfied, he pulled back onto the road and continued Northwest at three miles over the speed limit. It seemed like only a few moments had passed when he saw a sign with an arrow pointing left with US 62 West under it. As he approached the intersection the female voice said, "Bear left and proceed twenty nine point eight miles to the intersection of US 62 and CR122 South."

Dutch checked his rear view mirror and saw nothing coming from behind, traffic was very light, for that matter he did not remember seeing any traffic moving in the opposite direction for the last five minutes or so. "Well, it is ten o'clock in the morning," he mused.

Ten minutes later Johnny-one-eye's voice stated, "Take a hard right at the next intersection, there will be a wagon wheel hanging on a pole, go a mile and a half and take the dirt road to your left. Three miles in you will find a shack with a Coke sign on the roof, Rex will be there to meet you."

The wagon wheel was about one hundred and fifty feet in front of him, Dutch had about what seemed like a second to react to the new instructions, almost side swiping the pole as he slid around the corner throwing up a dust cloud that rose twenty feet in the air. "Son of a B......," the rear tires caught and the SUV jumped forward. Checking his rear view he saw nothing but the cloud of dust dispersing over the adjoining field. He drove about a mile and stopped, he checked the rear view mirror again to see if there were any other clouds of dust behind him. It would be impossible for any one following to not throw up a cloud. Looking around in a full circle he could see nothing out of place in any other direction of him for that matter. The air was clear and the sun was bright, the heat was ever present.

Continuing on he saw the dirt road that spurred off to his left, he took the turn slowly and proceeded at fifteen miles and hour in an attempt to keep the following dust cloud down. It still billowed up as high as the SUV and twice a long. As he breached one of the few rises in the road he saw the shack just ahead on his right. There was a cowboy Cadillac parked at the far side of the drive in front of the building, the '66' SS Chevy El Camino was covered with a light layer of dust. From its appearance it looked like it had been there for at least a few hours.

Dutch pulled next to the Chevy, leaving a space that about two cars could fill, and turned the SUV off. He did not get out, but sat watching the windows and the door of the shack for any movement. Two or three minutes passed before the door opened and a lone man stepped out onto the porch. The man was about six two or three, and looked to be of medium build, he wore jeans, dark green shirt and cowboy boots. The man's skin looked as hard, and wrinkled, as the leather of the boots he was wearing.

Dutch opened the door and stepped out, and away from the SUV, and with a nod walked towards the man saying, "Rex?"

The man stepped off of the porch and stopped about a foot and a half from Dutch replying, "Yep, you must be Dutch."

Dutch just smiled and nodded his head.

"Well, we need to talk a spell." Rex moved over towards his Chevy and put his foot up on the front tire. He reached into his shirt pocket and pulled out a pack of smokes. He offered the pack to Dutch.

"No thanks."

"Not a problem."

Dutch leaned against the front door of the Chevy saying, "Is there a problem with my friend?"

"Nope, just waiting for a call letting me know that all is clear and you both will be able to get out of here. It seems that there has been some kind of big city police and sheriff's office reaction to some explosion that happened earlier today. The Sheriff shut the airport down for a time, they mean to check out that everyone that is leaving town today, is who they are suppose to be. Seems that the four men that got killed this morning weren't who the documents they found said they were."

"I saw the news coverage of that earlier, six bodies were found, at least most of them anyway. Fire Captain said it was a Meth Lab."

Rex chuckled, "Yea that shit happens around here a lot. There are a lot of fools out there cooking that shit."

Dutch watched as he lifted his hand to take a drag of his smoke. He caught sight of a blur as Rex's foot was driven off of the Chevy's tire and Rex fell backwards away from Dutch.

A seven-foot rattlesnake was attached to Rex's boot. The force of the snake's strike was strong enough to drive Rex's foot off of the tire and knock him to the ground. In what seemed like a fraction of a second the snake was recoiling for a second strike.

The sound of the forty-five's discharging echoed off of the shack giving the impression of twin shots being fired. The bullet shattered the snake's head, leaving the body to twist and turn in an elaborate death dance. The body of the snake was as thick as the barrel of a Louisville Slugger.

Dutch was at Rex's side with his boot in his hands, almost before the echo died away, "Hey man, you okay?"

Rex pushed up on his elbows and with a grin on his face replied, "Think so, hell of a shot, man."

Dutch ignored the comment about the shot and asked, "Think he got through your boot?"

Pulling his boot out of Dutch's hands, and getting back on his feet, Rex replied "Nope, upper leathers quarter of an inch thick. There made to stop one of those guys from getting ya. He must have climbed up in there to keep warm, heard of it, but that's the first time I've ever seen it. He would have got me with that second strike. Big as he was, would have meant some serious time in the hospital, might even have lost something in the process." Putting out his hand he continued, "I owe you a big one, and remind me never to try to play gunslinger with you. I meant what I said, that was one hell of a shot."

Dutch shook his hand replying, "Lucky shot."

Rex replied, "Right, luck my ass," he stepped over to the snake's body and kicked it into the air with it landing about ten feet in front of his Chevy.

Dutch grinned, saying, "No Problem, glad I was

here to help. Now about that pick up I was to make. I'm sure that shot made someone nervous."

Rex pulled a cell phone from his pocket and turning towards the shack pushed a few buttons, he waved for Dutch to follow.

Chapter 23

RYAN STOOD NEXT TO HIS desk looking at the wall holding the phone to his ear, "Yes Sir, I'll be sure to give all of the men involved a 'Well done' from you. Yes Sir, we did catch a break not having anyone injured and very little collateral damage."

The Chief of Detectives continued, "Hell of a job Ryan, by the way, the Detective Lt. at the Fourteenth wants you to look at a body they have at the Central ME's office. He would like your help with the investigation of the case. I've also gotten a request to allow you to work with some new government group that's working out of the Borough of Richmond, You have my authorization to do so for both if you want to. If you don't tell them on second thought I disapproved the request.. Have a good day and Ryan, thanks again."

"Yes sir, thank you," A click was all that followed.

"Must be that thing Rebecca was talking about, and the other must be Danny's group." Ryan mused.

His P/C rang, signaling an incoming e-mail. He pushed the button on his mouse and opened the e-mail screen. The new e-mail was from Danny.

Ryan reread the short e-mail, "Billy, Urgent that you help. Talked to 1 Police Plaza, Okayed your involvement. Need a plan!" from his cousin Danny for the third time before he called him.

Just before the line connected he could hear the faint buzz that a scrambler produces. "

With out thinking, as soon as the connection completed, he asked "Danny, what's up cousin? Why the secure line?"

"Needed, Billy, remember that event that we discussed, the one that all were very concerned about, that might happen."

"Yes, what has changed?"

"Well, luckily, as you know, our dear cousins, Dutch and Freddie somehow have ended up in the middle of this mess."

"Freddie, I thought Dutch was leaving that alone."

"Billy, I know that you know a lot more than you are letting on. Even with his calls being scrambled we still have a record of the amount of time his phone was connected to yours over the past four or five days."

Ryan grinned to himself replying, "Think it might have been a wrong number?"

Danny laughed, "Right," he continued with, "like Dutch would listen to what anyone said. He was in Las Vegas and then Saint Louis and we finally tracked the two of them down in Albany. They were driving a vehicle with six different sets of license plates in the trunk. It seems the vehicle was a gift from an unknown source in Vegas. If Freddie hadn't slipped out and called his Mom, we never would have found them. Once he called we had a general location so we flooded the area with agents and found then driving down the interstate."

"Freddie is a klutz," Ryan said shaking his head.

"Right, I believe that Dutch was trying to get back to the city to meet with you and decide what the next move would be. In Albany he had a meeting with our people and the people from Homeland Security to explain what he recovered besides our unlucky cousin Freddie."

"Okay, yes, he was on the way here, but he never told me anything, just that when he got here we would need to contact a lot of people. Where is he now?"

Danny did not sound very happy as he continued, "He and Freddie are the guests of the Government in a five star hotel somewhere in the continental United States. It's my guess that they will be guests until this mess is over."

"What did Dutch find?" Ryan knew that his voice had taken on a very professional tone. He did not like it, Danny was blood.

"Well, Information, Freddie's business partners have made contact with a very unfriendly group of people and are close to making a purchase, with a price tag of One Hundred and Ten million dollars, cash American. The purchase and transfer of the very hot merchandise is to be out on the end of Long Island. As you know there are several long stretches of highway that run along the Sound and there has to be a hundred of little side roads that run down to the water and are desolate. The Navy and the Coast Guard are sure that they can find and capture the guys with the merchandise once they know the 'When' part of the equation."

"Well if their moving one hundred and ten million

you should be able to track them with your system. Right?"

"Right, but the sensors are twenty, and up to eighty, miles apart that far out on the expressway. There are a lot of those small roads in a twenty-mile stretch. Let alone eighty miles. It's our best guess that the transaction will happen during an evening rush hour, most likely on a Friday. That will prevent any large group of cars from traveling at high speed from happening. As you know the last forty miles or so of the expressway are open since most of the business travelers that live that far out travel by train. The early gridlock will act as a buffer for these guys. We need a way of getting a fairly large group of officers anywhere along that sixty six-mile stretch of highway. We need to recover the money but more importantly we need to take these guys alive. We're quite sure that they will be instructed to not let that happen."

Ryan responded, almost to himself, "One Hundred and Ten Million, and five or six bad guys, that will take up a lot of room. My guess is a delivery vehicle, like a step van or a couple of large SUV's of some sort. Either of those will not raise an eye out there no matter what time it goes down. I'm sure that they will have a front car and a chase car, both about a mile from the main group. They will use prepaid cell phones to stay in touch and have police scanners to stay informed of any police activity."

"Yes, that is what we came up with. Our problem is getting five or six vehicles full of well armed men to any location along that expressway, passing the lookout cars, without them broadcasting that were on the way. You know that the Government's Black SUV's will stick out like an elephant at a tea party. If these guys get spooked we're pretty sure that everything will go up in smoke with in several hundred feet of them."

"Well, Danny let me call you back in a few. I need to digest all of this. Do you have any idea what the time frame for when this will occur?"

"Billy, this could happen tomorrow, next week or next month. It is our best guess that it will happen Friday a week or the following week. We believe that for them to move the merchandise across the county to where we think the target is, and get access to it for set up, they will need to meet that time frame. Our guess is based on the schedule for an event, and return of someone, that we know is up coming that has been discussed in coded communications by people in the Middle East. This event will have international TV coverage and tens of thousands of people in one place. We truly believe that that event will be the target."

"I hope the event you are guessing is not the one I'm thinking about. I'll call you back." He pushed the End button not waiting for a response. Ryan sat back in his chair and stared up at the ceiling trying to concentrate on the events and problems that he wished he had not just heard. His eyes followed the cracks in the plaster as they stretched across the ceiling in random patterns. Leaning back towards his desk he picked up a pen and started to jot down his thoughts. He had a plan that he believed would get the forces where they needed to be with out much of a problem.

Chapter 24

ACKIE CAPONIA CLIPPED HIS CELL phone back into the holder on his belt shaking his head at the gullibility of people in general. As vice-president of American Insurance he was amassing a considerable fortune. The shell game played with the monies collected for the insurance policies that were sold and were continuing to be sold at bargain prices was bringing in tens of thousands a week.

Joanie, his office manager and assistant, was a workaholic that made everything seem on the up and up. She spent most of the day taking calls about claims and sending out checks to the few that meet all of the policies fine print. She always had a kind word and a recommendation of some government agency that might help the large group whose claims were disapproved. He got up and walked into the outer office and smiled at Joanie Callendello.

Joanie smiled at him and holding up a bank bag said, "Please don't forget to drop this off at the bank on your way to lunch."

"Got it, I'll be back later today. I've got to stop and see one of our clients, they'er behind on a payment."

"Okay, I'll hold down the ship."

Jackie smiled taking the bank bag and headed out the door. The client he had to see was Mrs. Rose Pattz, young, good looking, gullible, her husband in the hospital and deeply in debt. "It will be a good afternoon" he thought to himself.

Jackie stopped by the bank and walked to his loft to freshen up for his afternoon visit to Rose Pattz. He would explain how their insurance coverage was going to be dropped due to their not paying the extra insurance rider policy bill. He would explain that the extra coverage was needed due to the fact that they were near the point that they were exceeding the dollar limit of their coverage. He was sure that she would cry and explain how they could not afford any more insurance. He would offer to extend the coverage at no cost if she would show him how grateful she was. He had used this ploy many times in the past and always enjoyed the extra effort that was given to show their gratitude. "Yes it would be a good afternoon" he thought.

He admired the building his loft was in as he approached it, four floors, with each floor being a 3600 sq foot condominium overlooking the river. It was just three months ago when he bought the condo from one of the owners of American Insurance. He had paid four hundred thousand dollars cash. A great deal, the condo should have sold for almost four million dollars but with all of the monies staying within the company it made sense. The insurance business was good, very good. He walked into the lobby, and walked to the elevators. Reaching the elevator put his key into the slot marked fourth floor and turned it, the up arrow lit and the doors opened.

Jackie stepped out of the elevator into a small hall just off of his living room. The first thing any visitor would see is the twenty foot section of wall that was entirely glass with a magnificent view of the river, and the city skyline beyond it.

Just as Jackie stepped into the living room he was struck at the base of his skull with a black jack. He went down like a deflating balloon into a quivering heap. The two men that had been waiting for him each grabbed an arm and lifted him into a strait backed chair they had positioned at the far end of the room. The chair sat on the section of floor covered in imported marble that led to the fireplace that spread across the entire wall.

The men cut his jacket and shirt off of him before they strapped his arms and legs to the chair. One of the men unzipped his trousers and pulling out his seven inches of manhood pissed in Jackie's face. The warmth of the liquid brought him around and he started to yell out, a rag was forced into his mouth and tape wrapped all the way around his head so that the tape overlapped itself so that it would stick. Jackie's eyes went from one to the other and he did not recognize either of the men.

One of the men leaned close to his ear and spoke softly, "You will think that you have died once for each person you have cheated and persecuted. This will take a long time my friend, you will see the sun pass one last time."

Jackie pulled against his bonds to no avail, he watched the other man draw the tip of his knife across his forearm. The pain and the sight of his blood flowing hit him at the same tine and he screamed into the rag.

The two men were very practiced at their craft, they cut and cut until they reached a point where Jackie would pass out.

Jackie's phone, on the floor in what was left of his pants, would ring just about every fifteen minutes. The calls started around three thirty and continued until five o'clock. Joanie Callendello would start calling in the morning at eight thirty and would finally call the police at ten.

The men would wait and when he awoke they would start again, cutting what looked like small tic-tac-toe boards into his first layer of skin. They then would take tweezers and pull the small squares of skin off, slowly moving up one arm and down the other, then each of his legs. The sun dipped behind the buildings just as they started on his shoulders, continuing on to his stomach, neck, and face. Jackie passed out the final time just as they started on his cheek. He sat in a large pool of blood that had slowly seeped out of his body. He died of blood loss, shock and fear; the men never stopped grinning at him, never.

They had placed each of the small squares of skin into glass jars marked 'Insurance Payment, First Installment.' They put the jars on the small smoked glass topped English table in the hall, next to the elevators when they left.

They made sure not to touch anything nor step into the blood pool as they left. Making sure to clean what needed to be cleaned and taking everything they brought in with them as they left.

Stopping just outside of the building, standing in the glow of the street light one of the men pushed the buttons on the cell phone he had just purchased earlier that day.

When the phone connected he heard, "Yes?" and replied, "All is done." Then he walked over to the black metal railing, that protected all passers- by from falling into the river and flipped the cell phone out far enough to land into the water but not far enough to be noticed by anyone that might be watching or passing. The two men drifted away in different directions fading into the night like they were never there.

Big Frank sipped his glass of wine as he waited for the call to connect, "Hello."

"Sal, Frank, just wanted to let you know that the first phase of that job in the city we discussed, well it is completed."

"That is good news, thank you for calling." Sal hung up and sat back taking a sip of his brandy.

Chapter 25

---

*D*UTCH STOOD LOOKING OUT OF the hotel room's window seeing everything but seeing nothing. There had to be some way to get out of the situation that he found himself in. Being held under protective custody, even in a great hotel was less than acceptable. All of his efforts to help Freddie had done nothing but put him in the position to be out of pocket. There were events occurring that could change the lives of every person in the county and he was helpless to do anything about them.

Dutch looked over at Freddie and shook his head, Freddie was like having an over sized ten year old that never grew up and never thought anything out fully in their life. He had had to monitor every move he made, every moment of the day. He should have been the poster child for ADD. The first time Dutch had let him out of his sight, and control, Freddie called his mother to brag how he had gotten away from the bad guys. Freddie had no idea of what was going on or what could happen. The Feds had the call traced in moments, and it was less than twenty minutes after that Dutch and Freddie had been surrounded by FBI and Federal Marshalls. Game over!

Chapter 26

RYAN WAS PACING BACK AND forth in front of his desk with a death grip on his phone. His voice was all business and his tone was that of a cop.

"Okay Danny, I have a plan that will let thirty officers travel anywhere needed. Even if they have to go the full sixty six miles of the Long Island Expressway, they'll be able to do it in less than forty minutes if needed."

"Forty minutes, what will they be doing, flying?"

Ryan half laughed replying, "On wheels. Once you know the money is on the move release the Navy and Coast Guard. They need to find the boat that is carrying the merchandise without being found out or seen. They can move in on the boat just as we get the money and the guys with it."

"Okay, just how in the hell are we going to get thirty officers close enough to take over the bad guys and the money with out being seen by the lookout cars?"

We need to let them get well out on the Long Island Expressway. Your tracking system will give us their location at all times. Once we know that the boat is under surveillance an all points will be transmitted over the local and State Police radio bands, with continual up-dates, about the State Police in pursuit of a Corvette, traveling at speeds up to and exceeding one hundred miles an hour. Warning that the driver is armed and dangerous and wanted for raping and murdering the teenage daughter of a New York City Fireman. You need to get the State Police to lend you six or seven of those hopped up highway cruisers they keep up state. Make sure they put Island tags on them they can be waiting just off one of the on ramps in Long Island City. Make sure that the drivers are some of the troopers from up state also; the locals might flip out running at a hundred or more. Also broadcast the chase over all the channels of the CB band with updates every thirty seconds, the guys on the boat might pick that up."

"Well, its 43.4 miles from Long Island City to Islandia and another 3.6 miles to Holbrook. The Expressway is dead straight for fifteen or so miles in that area. We need to make the stop between Islandia and Holbrook, Long Island, there is a bridge for RT 93 that goes over the expressway about 1.8 miles out of Islandia towards Holbrook. The road narrows to two lanes in each direction with little or no shoulder. I checked that out this past weekend. The entire Expressway is only 66 miles long from Long Island City to its end at Baiting Hollow NY."

"What about the traffic on the road?"

"The police cars need to stay close so it looks like an army of lights flying at them to anyone looking in their rearview mirror. When the speeding cars fly by the "Out Car" they shouldn't raise any flags. I think the "Out Car and the Look Out" cars will be about two or three miles in each direction of the money vehicle so they have time to react if something comes up, Once the Vett and police cars go by the money vehicle and are out of sight of it, the Vett will slow and pull across the left lane and sticking part of the way in the right lane. Hopefully it will be close to RT93 and will be before they reach the lead" Look Out" car. The police cars will pull one in front of it, two behind it and the two of the other three will be on the right shoulder just past the Vett. That will leave a single lane open for traffic to move by in. The third one needs to go a quarter of a mile past and sit in the median to get the "Look Out" car if he decides to come back and save his Buddies. He'll know who it is because he'll be coming faster than the average speeder.

The Vett's driver will be being held down on the hood with his hands cuffed behind him. Lots and lots of flashing lights and howling sirens will cause all the traffic to funnel tightly into the right lane early. You know and I know that with the rubber necking the passing vehicles will be doing less than five miles and hour. The driver will bolt into the oncoming traffic just as the money vehicle is passing. The plan is for the Vett's driver to break away from the Vett and run into the side of the money vehicle with six to ten officers chasing him with their guns drawn. At the same time the officers on the shoulder side flatten the tires and bust open the windows and doors. The Navy and Coast Guard need to be released at the same time. That boat needs to be hit from the water and air at the exact same time. I think the Coast Guard should keep a watch at the area around Baiting Hollow Beach, that's as close as the Expressway gets to the water.

The surprise should make it all work. The one thing

that has to happen, Danny, Dutch needs to be the one driving the Vett."

"Billy the plan sounds like it will work and I can get everything done but there is no way that I can get Dutch released to do this."

"Danny, You and I both know that he's the only one that can pull this off in the short time we have to put it all together. He doesn't need to be trained and besides he's the only one I'll let drive my Vett at speeds over a hundred miles an hour."

"Okay, I'll run the whole thing past the powers to be and get back to you as soon as I can."

"Good, Danny, give my best home." Ryan ended the call before he heard the reply.

Chapter 27

DANNY PULLED INTO THE PARKING lot of the small strip mall that sat a block off of the most north western stretch of Highland Boulevard, just before you came to the channel between the island and New Jersey. There were what seemed to be five small business offices in the mall. One was a closed Doctor's office, with a sign on the front that hung at a forty five degree angle, announcing the moving to Prince's Bay. Another was an emergency veterinary clinic also with a We've moved sign, with yet another specializing in discount shoe sales. The two in the rear of the building had for rent signs taped across the entrances with the glass doors covered with brown paper.

He walked into the shoe store and walked directly to the rear of the store where he was concealed from the windows and door of the store. He waited for a few moments and heard the song born free start to play on the store speakers. He opened the door on the rear wall and stepped into a small hallway. He faced three doors and he opened the middle one and stepped in. There was a twenty by twenty room with a round table in the middle.

There were three men sitting at the table and one of the men stood and motioned for Danny to take a seat at the table. Once he was seated the only man wearing a suit began to speak. "We are at a very difficult time gentlemen, very difficult. We have it on very good intelligence that there will be a delivery of 'Red Mercury' on Long Island within the next two weeks.

One of the other men questioned, "The Sam Cohen's 'Red Mercury?'"

"Yes."

The remaining man asked, "Do we know where it this coming from?"

"Yes, South Africa."

Danny spoke up looking at the men sitting before him, "I'm sorry but I do not have a clue what you are talking about."

The man in the suit looked at him and began to speak slowly and grimly, "Sorry, what we are talking about is 'Red Mercury', the matter needed to make a Neutron Bomb. Mr. Sam Cohen is the leading expert on this subject in the world. Every President of the United States since Truman has been trying to ignore him and his concerns. It is known that there were large amounts of 'Red Mercury' made in Russia and sold on the black market for years. It is believed that China has a stock pile of Neutron Bombs and so does the defunct 'White Government of South Africa.'

The second man that spoke continued, "An amount the size of a major league hardball can kill everything within a three city block area, people, animals, insects, everything. The shipment to be received is comprised of three thirty gallon drums weighing one hundred and seventy five pounds each."

"My God, if it was all to be used at one time an entire city would be void of life, even a city the size of New York.

"Gentlemen, no matter what happens, no matter what must be done this shipment must be stopped. The entire governments support is on the table, money, all departments, Army, Navy, Air Force. Coast Guard, everything and anything!

They sat there looking at their hands, Danny began to speak, "I have a plan that was put together by my cousin, Detective Lieutenant William Ryan of the New York City Police Department."

"How in the hell did a local cop find out about what is going on?"

"Are you telling me with all of the United States capabilities the only thing we have is a plan from a New York cop?"

Danny started again, "Let me tell you the events that have brought me to this meeting. Up until three hours ago I did not even know any of you existed."

"Well, let's hear it, we need something."

"Yes, let's hear it."

With that Danny started from his receiving the first call about Freddie and the insurance fraud. He left out the names of the people in his family, all of the members except Freddie, Dutch and Billy. He went over Billy's plan for the recovery of the money and the contraband at the same time.

They all sat there for a few moments digesting what they had just heard and the man with the suit stood and stepped to the far corner of the room and taking out a cell phone spoke in soft murmurs. He stepped back to the table, and sitting, looked around at the men surrounding him stopping at Danny saying, "You have the World's forces and wealth at your service. You must present and implement your plan, and what each and every support group must do and when. A meeting is being set up for six tomorrow morning that will be top secret and you will be in charge. Have whoever you want with you at your house at five in the morning. Transportation to the meeting will be handled. You have complete authority over everything and anything you want and/or need. Put who ever, in whatever position you want, just get this done."

With that said the man with the suit and one of the other men stood and left the room. Danny stood there with a stunned look on his face feeling numb. The remaining man looked at him and stated, "The next few weeks will be the toughest of your life." He then turned and left the room.

Danny stood there for a few moments and then walked out of the room and through the shoe store and to his car.

Chapter 28

RYAN PULLED HIS CAR INTO the reserved space next to the over sized space with the bright red sign marked, MEDICAL EXAMINER. Rebecca's car was in the space and from the looks of the parking job she parked in a hurry. He walked up to the main door and pushed the alert button and the security officer opened the door. He put his revolver in a plastic bowl with his watch and money clip before stepping through the metal detectors.

He smiled to himself thinking about how much things had changed in a short time, not but a few years ago anyone could walk into the building and lab with not so much as a "Who are you?' being said.

He collected all of his items and putting them in place headed for the main lab entrance. Entering he saw Rebecca standing by the sixth examining area down talking with one of the many people in the room in white lab coats. He moved in that direction being sure to stay outside of the red lines that marked the floor. Each line was a good as an eight foot wall.

Rebecca looked up and saw him coming, she ended

her conversation with the tech and smiling stepped towards her husband. She pulled his close and gave him a peck on the cheek saying, "Hi, love you."

Ryan replied, "Love you more."

Stepping back and taking a business stance he asked, "What have we got? You said you had something for me to look at and the Fourteenth told the Captain of D's that I had to look at something for them also .Are they both the same thing?

Rebecca switched back to her professional mode in an instant, "No, if you step over here I'll show you the one that is bothering me." She moved to the West wall of the lab and, opening one of the cooler doors, pulled and slid out one of the examining tables with a cadaver on it.

The body was that of a young woman, the tag on her toe read Jane Doe, she was maybe twenty something, with the marks of an autopsy.

Ryan looked at Rebecca with a questioning look on his face, they had seen hundreds of Jane Doe's and asked, "What am I looking for?"

"Well, Bill that's just it. There are no signs of lone term drug use, alcohol use, prostitution, slavery, beatings, nothing, no abuse of any sort. Yet here she is on one of my slabs with nothing but the signs of giving birth recently and in perfect health. She is the fourth one in about twenty months that I know of. There might be more in the sub morgues out in the boroughs."

He looked at Rebecca and after s few moments replied, "How do we tie them together and what do I take to Police One to have them open a case?"

Rebecca's shoulders sagged a bit, as she replied, "I

do not have a clue Bill, but there is something bad, very bad going on out there."

He put his arm around her saying, "I'll see what I can do."

"Thanks."

"What was the one that the Fourteenth caught?

She placed her hand on his arm and led him seven rows of drawers further down the wall. Pulling open the door and the slab he was looking down at a thirty something male about six two and two twenty.

"Big guy, what's the scoop?"

"Well, according to Detective Cirrilo he was a Private Security Guard, on his way to work sometime around three twenty yesterday. Someone used something to cut through his rib cage and cut his heart in two, it killed him instantly. Whatever was used to kill him was big and very, very sharp, cut the bone cleanly and left no marks that a knife would normally leave. He was found on the subway station floor, he was apparently heading for the steps to go out to the street and to work. He was found in a puddle of bloody water and my investigators found nothing, no foreign objects of any kind. My autopsy found no weapon marks of any kind, other than the gaping wound in his chest, the cause of, I have no clue. He was found five minutes after the last train left the station and ten minutes before the next one arrived. The station security cameras were damaged and did not work and there was no one at the station at the time of the incident so there is nothing to go on. And that love is why they want you to get involved."

"Well this is great, dead woman with no cause of death to be found and a guy big enough to play with the Jets found with his chest cut open by magic with no signs of a struggle and there are no clues to either, I guess I hit the jackpot."

"Oh, buy the way, I have a class tonight so I'll be late."

"Great" He stepped a little closer to Rebecca and whispered, "How would you like to run away with me for a few hours, maybe this will all go away."

She laughed stepping away saying, "Not me buddy, you're not getting me involved in any of this. I'm going to my office and read a few files. See you tonight."

He took a false step her way and she waved as she hurried into her office. He pulled out his phone as he headed for the door. He scanned his contact list for Cirrilo's number, finding it hit the call button.

"Cirrilo."

"Ryan, send me a copy of the five on the security guard and let me know if anything comes up."

"You got it, things good?"

He replied, "Past Twenty Five" with a chuckle.

The phrase "Past Twenty Five" meant he was with the department longer that twenty five years and could retire any time he wanted to. It also gave him a lot of breathing room when things got a little tight with the Brass.

"Thanks Lou."

Bill put the phone back into its holder and before he reached his car it beeped again. He put it to his ear and said, "Ryan."

"Billy, this is Uncle Joe Patillo."

"Uncle Joe, how are you, how is Aunt Patsy?"

"She is good, I need to talk to you, you know, just us."

"Okay Uncle Joe, I can meet you tomorrow for lunch and ….."

"No, No it needs to be now. Please Billy."

"Okay, where are you now?"

"Uncle Sammy's place, the one on 21st Street."

"Okay, I'll be there in fifteen minutes or so."

Ryan started the car and called in letting the dispatcher know that he was leaving the Medical Examiner's Office and taking a 10/10 for an hour or so. He drove to his Uncle Sammy's store and once he parked walked across the street and into the store. As he entered he saw his Uncle Joe standing next to a young man that stood about six feet seven inches tall and looked about four feet wide.

He walked over with his hand out to shake his uncle's hand; his uncle pushed his hand aside and gave him a hug and saying, "We knew you would help, we knew."

Ryan stepped back a bit and looking at his Uncle and said, "Uncle Joe what is this all about, help how? What is wrong?"

His Uncle put his hand on the young man's arm and said. "This is my son, your cousin Jerry, you remember him? He was small the last time you saw him, you know size wise. Now he plays for Rutgers, you know football. Billy, the Pro's, they want him, very much, very much so."

"Uncle Joe, that's great but I don't understand what I'm here for."

Jerry put his hand on his father's shoulder and then put it out for Ryan to shake it.

Ryan took the offered hand and shook it.

Jerry made a motion towards the chairs sitting along the wall. "Why don't we sit down," once seated Jerry continued, "Officer Ryan, I need to ….."

Ryan lifted his hand, "Billy, its Billy, Cousin Jerry."

Jerry turned a little red and continued, "Billy, I signed a contract with the Giants four months ago to play linebacker. They gave me a five year contract for six million dollars, I'm sure you did not see anything about it with all of the fifty and seventy million contracts that were flying around. Well six million is more than I ever thought I would make in a life time let alone five years.

"Jerry that is wonderful, but I still don't understand."

"Well Billy, Recently I was contacted by an Attorney about a paternity suit and he wants me to take a DNA test. Some lady has named me the father of her soon to be born child and in the paternity suit. The suit spells out the conditions for me to pay five thousand dollars a month cash until the child is out of college."

Ryan shook his head and repeated, "Jerry I'm still in the dark. If you had relations with someone and she got pregnant you have the responsibility to support the child."

Jerry stood up and paced two strides and turned back taking two strides, he stopped and faced Ryan saying, "I agree with you completely but that is just it, I've never had relations with anyone." His face was now as red as a stop light. "I was brought up with the belief that you waited until you were married and you can believe that or not, but I live by that. The Attorney contacted me and said the test came back positive, I know that is not possible."

Ryan sat back in the chair and tried to digest what he had just heard.

Jerry opened his jacket and took a manila folder out

and handed it to Ryan, "This is a copy of everything I have concerning this whole thing. All I'm asking is that you look at it and give me some advice, if you see fit."

Ryan stood and facing Jerry took the folder saying, "I'll look at it, no promises, but I will take a long look at it."

Jerry put his hand out again and said, "That is all I can ask, thank you." He shook Ryan's hand and looked at his father and grinning said, "Okay, Pop, let's go."

Ryan's Uncle grasped his hand with both of his and said, "Thank you Billy, Thank you." He and his son moved towards the door, Jerry had his arm around his father's shoulders and he hardly had to raise it above his waist.

Ryan watched them leave and watched his Uncle Sammy walk into the store. His Uncle walked over and shook Ryan's hand and said, "Whatever it is, thank you for helping, Joe is really shook up."

Ryan started towards the door and replied, "I'll do what I can, Uncle, my best home."

A thank you followed him out of the door.

He was just reaching for the car door when his phone rang again. He opened it with, "Ryan."

"Billy, you need to be at my house tonight. We have a meeting at six o'clock in the morning. That is all I can say until you get here." Danny never waited for his cousin to answer he just hung up hoping that would put the importance in the call.

Ryan stood there looking at his phone, "What the hell." He pushed the button until he got to Slim's number. He pushed 'Send.'

Rebecca picked up the phone and replied, "Yes, sweetheart."

"Slim, I have to spend the night at Danny's, I'll know more once I get there."

"Okay, my class gets out late so I will not get home until eleven or so, call after eleven thirty."

"Okay, talk to you later, love you."

"Love you."

Ryan got into the car and starting it and headed home, picking up the radio handset he keyed the mike saying, "Ryan, I'll be at the house in twenty minutes."

Once he reached his place he entered and hurried to put a change of clothes in a bag and made sure he put his toiletries in the bag also. It was less than fifteen minutes and he was on his way to the precinct house.

Chapter 29

---

*R*EBECCA PICKED UP THE ARTICLE that she needed to finish reading to be prepared for her class in a few hours. What is DNA? The article was written by her professor and read like DNA for Dummies! She had not been impressed with the first few classes and unless something improved she might not finish the first class in her entire educational experience to date. She turned the first page and made herself read the information before her even though it was data she already knew.

DNA – (Deoxyribonucleic acid) is the genetic material in every cell. There are 46 chromosomes in each human cell, apart from those in sperm cells and egg cells, which have only 23 chromosomes. The 46 are attained at the moment of conception, the two sets combine to make the 46 necessary to create a person.

DNA is the most powerful and advanced technique for identification and also in determining paternity. It's testing has a degree of certainty of between 99.9% and 100% which is accepted by US Courts as absolute proof of identity and or paternity.

Rebecca shook her head, nothing that she did not know already, just basic stuff.

She turned the page and on the back was the bio of her professor, it caught her interest. More so then the man himself had so far.

Dr. David S. Stevens, MD

Department Head - of the New York Institute for the advancement of Medical Research, specializing in the fields of DNA and Reproduction Techniques.

The world's leading practitioner in the field of artificial insemination and a leader in the area of cell cloning.

A list of his published papers filled almost three quarters of the page.

The article's bio went on to list the list of important's that he had assisted in their quest to become parents. It also listed his successes with the cloning of cells, both animal and human.

"Well, maybe I have to give him a second chance. The class is open to anyone so I guess he would need to start slow. We'll see." Rebecca mused to herself.

Chapter 30

BARRY LOOKED OUT THE WINDOW and saw the police car at the rear door of the building next door and the two plains clothes officers were questioning the three security guards that stood around them like puppies. He grinned and glanced back at his computer screen and almost laughed at the list of over 100 different places where useless beings could be found to be picked for his purging. He realized that he must select beings from varied places with his true targets scattered amongst the rubble he would leave behind. The police got back into their car and pulled away leaving the security guards standing there watching the dust from their tires settle.

His computer pinged and Barry almost jumped out of his skin, "Can't do that, no, no must pay attention. Time to go hunting, must get at least one tonight, at least one." He walked to the rear door and opened it and scanned the entire parking lot. He knew the police had left but he must be careful, very careful. Seeing nothing that made him uncomfortable he walked quickly to his car and getting in locked the door quickly. In moments he was on his way home, his plan was to visit the Avenue of the America's before dinner.

Pulling into his garage and watching the door securely close he unlocked the car door and exited. He went directly to the kitchen and pulled the basket out of the closet that held all of his tools. He took the Freezesac out of the basket and walked over to the freezer. He put one of the four swords that he had ready into the sac. He swung the Freezesac strap over his shoulder and then pulled the trench coat over it. He was so excited that he could hardly contain himself; he rushed to the door and in moments was on the subway heading up town. It took him about thirty moments and two trains to get him to the destination he had selected. He walked half a block west and stepped into an alley and walked in about twenty paces where he found an entrance door on each wall giving him access to either building. He put on his gloves and randomly picked the door to his left, finding the door unlocked. He entered the building and moved quietly towards the front entrance, stopping at the walls end but staying behind it and out of sight.

Barry heard the front door being opened and un-zipped the Freezesac and took out the sword. He stepped around the corner and standing before him was a young woman about thirty four year old. She turned towards him with a look of surprise and before she could say a word, the sword cut through the pretty pink dress that she was wearing and split her ribs and heart. She was dead before she hit the floor.

Barry turned and moved retracing his steps and was leaving the alley behind him as someone discovered the young woman's body, as announced by a scream.

With a smile on his face Barry followed his path

in reverse and upon his arriving home poured himself a tall glass of milk, he toasted himself on another successful trip. He was the happiest man in the city at this point in his life. He, and only he, was culling the herd, the second one tonight must not be one of the subject targets just another chunk of rubble. Tomorrow he would get his second target, yes tomorrow.

He just could not wait another second he had waited about an hour and knew he was going out again; he was just amazed that the effort to complete his tasks was so easy, soooooo easy! Ah, and the sword just slides right in there, yes, yes, right in there.

Barry washed up and cooked himself a small meal, he had to keep his strength up now that he had the power. He waited until eight o'clock and donned his hunting gear and headed out the door, he had made sure not to watch the news. He would wait until the eleven o'clock news and see the results of his culling two from the herd.

He walked across town a few blocks and took the subway up-town again, only this time he rode for over forty minutes before he left the train. He walked a block and a half west and again stepped into and alley. He put on his gloves and slowly searched the alley for the rear doors that he knew were there hidden in the grayness, he again found two doors but both were locked. He stepped back and looked for any lighted windows that faced the door from the adjoining building. There were none so he stepped back to the door and popped the glass out and reached in and unlocked the door. He realized that he would have to do something to get one of the residents to come out of their apartment without raising the entire building. He moved along the hall to the main lobby and stood in front of the list of names and door bells. He passed over all of the Mr. and Mrs. And found two on the first floor that only had single names. He press one and a male voice responded "Yes?"

"Please help me, please help me, please help,,,,!" He whispered urgently.

Barry quickly stepped back against the wall, just as he got into position he hear a door open. He un-zippered the sac and pulled out the sword. In a moment a large shape stepped to the doorway looking towards the call buttons, Barry stepped forward and drove the sword through the man's rib cage from the back with an upward thrust. It burst through the ribs and entered the heart continuing its trip till the tip protruded through the skin of the man's chest. He collapsed like an empty sack, dead before he hit the floor just as all of the others had fallen.

Barry turned and rushed back along the path he had taken entering and soon found himself moving down the sidewalk away from yet another wonderful experience.

He thought about his previous goal of one a week and laughed to himself, "One a week, ha. Maybe ten a week or even twenty, hell this is fun. Next it would be another rent a cop, "They will come to know, 'Paybacks are a bitch."

Chapter 31

*S*AL WAS STANDING BACK ADMIRING one of the many display cases that held his collections of Lladro figures, he had just placed the newest one on the middle shelf, and center stage where it would remain until the next took its place. The cell phone in his pocket vibrated breaking the wonderful feeling of contentment that one falls into when all seems right. The vibrating signal was letting him know he was not alone and all is not always well. Pushing the lit button he said, "Yes?"

A voice on the other end said, "That problem that I have been watching, it is time to complete the actions that were discussed, the problem has found a pattern that is being repeated."

"Do what you must." Sal turned off the phone and put it back in his pocket. He looked at the case and the light hearted feeling he had had was gone. Putting his hands in his pockets he moved slowly into the living area of his home and found some solace in the comfort of his recliner.

The caller put the phone in his pocket and remained standing in the shadows of the buildings that surrounded the alley. He watched as Kumar-Kaffe left his building and entered the car that was waiting. He watched the car pull away from the curb and disappear around the corner heading up town. He waited five minutes and then moved slowly back into the depths of the alley and the exit that he knew waited at the end of the anchor fence that was installed to seal the alley. Reaching the fences end he pulled at the fencing and it moved away from the adjoining building allowing him passage. He walked across the street and down two blocks before quickly pulling open the door of the recently stolen car and getting in. Starting the car he pulled away, and drove three blocks west, and then turned left and up town. He drove for about fifteen minutes to go the eleven blocks he needed to go and turned east and went one block and took the first parking space he found. It really did not matter for he would never see the car again. He got out and continued walking eastward, he pulled the phone out of his pocket and dialed a number, it rang twice.

"What!"

"It is time!"

"Be there in ten minutes, I will come up the back."

"Yes." He walked a block and a half further and saw the car that Kumar-Kaffe had gotten into and the driver sitting behind the wheel in the middle of the next block. Just like he had seen every other night for the last three weeks, "Everyone has a pattern, everyone," he mused.

He walked to the front door of the brownstone and entered without being noticed by the driver. At that he smiled to himself, good help was almost impossible to find. He moved up the stairs to the third floor apartment and waited at the door. He got down on one knee and pretended to be tying his shoe laces should anyone appear from one of the other units on the floor. He heard a small cracking of glass and the scuffling of shoes moving towards him. Just as the door opened he rose driving his shoulder into the stomach of the man attempting to exit. The force drove both men into the apartment and he could hear the breath being driven out of the smaller man as he landed on top of him. His partner, who had entered by breaking one of the windows at the fire escape, and driving their prey out the door, closed the hall door and places his foot on Kumar-Kaffe's hair. There was still blood dripping from his arm, when he cut the woman's throat ,who had sat in the bed screaming, the blood had squirted all over his arm.

They placed several layers of tape over Kumar-Kaffe's mouth and bound his hands with wire with it, also circling it around his neck. The wire was strong enough to hold him, but thin enough to cut; any struggling just allowed the wire to cut deeper into his wrists and neck. They used heavy tape to bind his legs to a wooden straight back chair and the chair to the radiator attached to the heating system.

The second man reached out onto the fire escape platform and pulled in the large canvas bag that he had left there. He placed it in front of Kumar-Kaffe and slapped his face until his eyes filled with tears. Laughing he opened the bag and pulled out a piglet that weighed about twelve pounds. The Piglet was drugged and moved as if in slow motion, its mouth had been glued shut with crazy glue, and the only noise it could make was to snort.

Kumar-Kaffe felt the waves of panic pass through

him and his mind began the process of blanking out the thoughts that now exploded in his mind.

The first man lifted the piglet up right in front of Kumar-Kaffe's face and the second man made a cut along the body. The blood spilled onto Kumar's chest and lap.

He lurched forward so violently that the wire around his neck cut to the bones in his vertebra. His head lay to the side almost completely removed; the men cut the piglet up and stuffed his organs into Kumar's mouth and neck. They took the intestines and rapped them around his head like a turban and just laid the rest of the parts on his lap.

They both left by way of the window moving under the cover of the graying sky and remaining shadows that moved across the building.

The first man took a prepaid cell phone out of his pocket and called 911, he gave them his address and complaining of screams and loud noises coming from the floor above his. His second call was to the newspapers explaining of the complaint of what looked like a man and woman having sex in the window of their apartment and there were what looked like body parts on the street below the window.

As they walked down the adjoining street he pulled the Sim card out of the phone and dropped the phone down the sewer grate. He popped the Sim card into his mouth and chewed on it for a while spitting out what ever pieces that came loose. He did not need to make a confirming call about his work being done; the eleven o'clock news would do that for him.

Chapter 32

REBECCA WALKED INTO THEIR HOME and once she closed the door she made sure the twin locks were in place, it would be the first thing Bill asked her. She walked into the bedroom and changed into some sweats. Once in the kitchen she checked the refrigerator and took out the container left over pasta with meat sauce. She put it in the oven at three hundred degrees and then pulled a roll out of the bread box to have with the meal. She took a glass out of the cabinet, and opening the bottle of red wine that was on the counter and filled it. She put the glass of wine, roll, knife and fork on the table, the beep went off signaling that the pasta was done. She placed a pot holder on the table and then using two others took the pasta out of the oven and placed it on the pot holder on the table.

She sat down just as the phone rang, she answered with a "Hello Sweetheart."

"Hello love how was class?"

"Okay, it should get better."

Bill gave her a condensed and sterilized version of the events of the day. She could tell that he was just filling time and was saying most of what he was saying for who is whoever was eavesdropping. As she listened she picked up the folder that Bill had left on the table when he stopped home to get his clothes. She leafed through the pages and was surprised at the reports that were there.

"Bill, what is this folder about that you left on the table?"

"Folder, oh, great it's there, I didn't remember where I left it. I'll tell you about it when I get home tomorrow. It's a family thing."

"Okay, there are a few things that have caught my interest we need to discuss. Sleep well and be safe, I'll see you tomorrow evening.

"Slim, you also, make sure the locks are in place. Love you."

She smiled as she pushed the End button.

She read each and every paper in the folder; the papers from the Attorney really caught her eye. The Attorney's name was Donald S. Stevens, Rebecca's teacher is Dr. David S. Stevens and their addresses are in the same building.

The fact that the suit was a paternity suit and Dr. Stevens was a world renowned specialist in that field. Well, that is way too much of a coincidence, way too much.

Chapter 33

*D*ANNY AND BILL WERE WHISKED out of Danny's house at five fifteen in the morning under the cover of darkness and the auto crash that was staged as a diversion. They were moved to the arena where the county held kids programs on weekends. Arts and Crafts, Boy and Girl Scouts all kinds of Community activities.

The meeting was attended by men and women of the most important offices in the government, city, county, state, federal, everyone. Sitting on the stage were Danny and Bill, and Danny had just outlined the plan to recover the matter being smuggled into the country and the money stolen to pay for it. There was not a sound, nor a question just almost a hundred faces looking up at them. Each person sat there, waiting for their direction, their marching orders so to speak. It was explained that the plan was the plan, if you could improve it, speak up, otherwise find out what was expected of you and do it, do it right.

Every person was instructed that there would only ten to fifteen minutes to get everything in place and in motion. That meant that there would be almost three hundred people ready to react at a moment's notice.

Danny's phone beeped and the number that showed was that of the lead detective of his old precinct.

He flipped the phone open saying, "Danny."

"Danny, a heads up, Kumar-Kaffe was just found killed, it was really bad. Really, really bad. Whoever did it wrapped him in pig body parts and covered him in pig's blood. The media is going nuts."

"Thanks."

Danny sat there and just stared out into space.

Ryan touched his cousin's arm saying, "What's up?"

"I don't know how this is going to change what's going to happen but Kumar-Kaffe was just found killed and in a way to cast severe dispersion on his religion. It has been believed that he was not really in charge but just a figure head. If that is correct then the operation will still go ahead."

"Well all we can do is wait and see. I'm heading back into the city. Any Idea when Dutch will be here?"

He should be waiting for you at your office when you get there, fill him in for me. Oh, Freddie will be staying with some "friends" in Vermont until this is all over. He will be going to a minimum security prison for a year for his actions concerning the insurance policies. When this is over I'll meet with his Mother and explain it all."

"Great, I'll get Dutch up to speed," with that Bill pulled the hood of his Giant's hoodie over his head and moved out the side door and away from the mass of people that Danny had still to deal with.

Chapter 34

*B*ARRY SAT THERE GLUED TO the TV screen the images jumped off the screen, the glare of the TV lights made everything look so stark. The blood pool looks as black as tar and the pool seemed to cover the entire entrance hall floor. The body looked rumpled and very un-clean and the shirt and pants had rips and tears, the announcer speculates that the victim was a bag person that was attempting to break in to one of the apartments.

He explained how a bag person would enter an entrance hall and start pushing one apartment button per floor starting from the top. This is done with the expectation that someone will push the access button without asking who it is. They push one per floor so the neighbors would not hear the others ringing. Once the access lock is released they have free access to the entire building. Some just find the basement for a safe place to stay but others roam the halls listening at the doors for the sound of an easy mark. They love to hear the sound of a wheelchair or cane, easy and not capable of protecting themselves. The announcer was getting worked up and his voice got louder, "These are the scum of the earth, to them nothing is sacred and no one is safe."

The screen switched to a commercial.

Barry was not happy, not one word about the killer and his skills, it should be all about the killer. No, not a word, just a bunch of crap, crap about the bag guy the damn bag guy. "Well, I'll give them something to talk about and it will not be some damn bag guy."

He almost ran to the work room. He put the Freezesac on and moved over to the freezer. He opened the door and looked at his swords, there were fifteen in all, it made him smile. He took one and placed it in the sac and carefully closed the sac. He put the jacket on and was going out the door before he had it zipped up.

Barry walked across the street and walked down the stairs into the subway station on to the platform. He took the first train and got off at the second stop, he had no plan now it was more like a mission. He climbed the steps and walked uptown for two blocks and realized that there were very few people walking the street. He turned into an alley and walked towards the back. He was about twenty feet into the alley when he felt rather than saw the other person in the alley. He could tell that the person was behind him and the sounds led him to believe that they were moving towards him. He slowly unzipped the sac and took the sword out holding it in front of him. He turned quickly and saw that the stalker was just a few feet from him. His movements seemed to startle the stalker, Barry lunged forward thrusting the sword at the chest area of his would be attacker. The sword plunged in the man's chest and the extra force from the lunge drove the sword in all the way to the hilt. Barry stumbled directly into the man and they both fell backwards. Barry ended lying on top of the man, blood spurt from his chest like the spray from a hose. Barry stood as quickly as he could and looking down at his jacket and saw that it was covered with blood splatter. "Oh shit, oh shit, this is not good." Barry moved closer to the wall so that he would not be so noticeable from the street should a passerby glance down the alley. He stood there thinking of what he needed to do now. He stood there for a few moments and then took his jacket off and turned it inside out. He put it back on and knowing he needed to see as few people as possible decided to walk home. He moved to the end of the alley and stepped out and moved downtown at a normal pace without turning to look back or to look rushed. He looked at his reflection in the store windows reflection trying to assess just how bad he looked. It disturbed him that the blood had splattered onto his pants as well as his jacket. He knew that if he did not stop walking and stayed away from the brightest lit streets he should be alright.

He was an hour or so into his walk and he was still four blocks from home, this was going to be the hardest part of the trip. People here knew him and if they saw him walking where he did not frequent they would remember and surely look more closely at him. He had avoided any contact so far but he had to walk past the two empty lots that everyone within four square blocks used as their private pet toilet. If he got close to any of the dogs they would smell the blood and their actions would change from normal to abnormal. The change would make his passing memorable and should they ever be questioned it would stand out.

He stood on the corner for a few moments and made

the decision that the best course of action was to just do it. He stepped off and walked at a brisk pace keeping a sharp eye out for anyone that might be out and about. It took seven minutes for him to reach his door. He opened it and stepped in, closing the door firmly he slipped down the wall onto the floor where he shook violently.

He did not know if the shakes were just relief or a complete breakdown of his nervous system. Some time passed before he picked himself up off the floor and moved into the work area.

As he walked he scolded himself, "Never again, never ever go without a plan. I must always have a plan, think, think, think."

Once in the room he took off his jacket, the sac, shirt, shoes, socks, pants and underwear. He moved over to one of the cabinets and removed a large black plastic bag. He stepped back to his pile of clothing and stuffed all of them into the black bag. He used his shirt to wipe the floor, even though he did not see any stains. He closed the bag and tied it closed then walked over and placed it by the door to the garage area. He went to the cabinet that held the cleaning supplies and removed the bottle of spray bleach that he used to clean the floor. Barry placed the sac on the work table and sprayed it heavily with the bleach then he scrubbed it down with cleanser. Once he felt comfortable he stuffed the paper towels in the plastic bag and re closed it. He then walked back to the front door and wiped down the wall and floor just in case some blood inadvertently got on either.

He put everything back in its place and hurried into the living area. He made sure that he touched as little as possible and went directly into the shower. While the shower water softly rained down on him it hit him. As bad as it went tonight it might be the one that causes the most news coverage. He knew that there were signs of a struggle, so every square inch of the alley would be gone over with a fine tooth comb. He had not seen any surveillance cameras but there could have been one as far as a block away. The next few hours of news reports should be very, very interesting; the news people should be very busy gathering and tell the world all the things they should not. He turned the shower off and stepped out and toweled off. He dressed quickly and moved back into the living area.

He turned the flat screen on and there it was a special report on the 'Water Killer.' 'Water Killer' wow, Barry had gotten a title, wow, the photos of the alley, the victim and the blood pool kept flashing across the screen. The news announcer was babbling on and on about how this was the fourth killing, with all of the victims having their hearts split in two causing instantaneous death.

Chapter 35

*R*YAN GOT OUT OF HIS car and walked into the precinct house fully knowing that he would have so little personal time over the next few weeks. He had gotten a call from Slim about the information in the folder that Jerry had given him. She had a hunch that there was some connection between her professor and the Attorney that served Jerry the paternity suit. Sounded interesting but his plate was full right now, family stuff would have to wait.

Walking into his office he was not surprised to find Dutch sitting behind his desk working on his PC. "Hope that's business."

Dutch grinned as he stood up and started to move around the desk saying, "Well someone has to do some work on that thing."

They hugged and laughing Ryan said, "Just on Mondays and Fridays."

Ryan sat in his seat and Dutch pulled one of the other chairs up to the front of the desk. Ryan began to tell Dutch the entire course of events that had unfolded since he was picked up by the Feds. They talked for over an hour and Dutch convinced Ryan about a few changes but the plan remained basically the same. The changes would stay between them and did not need to be explained to Danny and the large group of people now involved.

Dutch stood and stretched his arms above his head saying, "I am taking a walk uptown to get a room. I also need to see a few people on the street and find out what the scuttlebutt is. I'll call with the details of who, what, where and when."

Ryan grinned and replied, "Sounds good, be ready to move at a moment's notice. Danny and his department, the Coast Guard, the Navy and NASA are scanning and searching every boat and vehicle that is moving anywhere to, on or from Long Island and the two hundred mile area surrounding it.

"You got it, let you know where I am as soon as I do." He turned and walked out the door just as Ryan's phone began to buzz.

Ryan answered saying, "Ryan."

"Ryan, this is Cirrilo."

Ryan waved at Dutch saying, "Yes, Cirrilo, what have you got."

"Well, we are up to four bodies, same wounds, same dead and no clues and no suspect. The only thing I've got is the media who has given this shit a tag name, Water Killer, believe it or not they are saying that theses Perps are being killed with ice."

"Ice, what does the Medical Examiner say about that?"

"Says it can be done, does not know how, but it can be done. Ice can hold a sharper edge than a knife blade. How the hell you move it and keep it from melting is another story."

"I'm neck deep in something right now but send me everything in an e-mail and I'll look it all over and get back to you."

"Thanks Lou."

He closed his phone and set it on his desk, Ryan stared at the wall and closed his eyes, and it seemed that he was being stretched four ways from the center.

His phone began to buzz.

He leaned over and picked it up, pushing the button he replied, "Ryan."

"Ryan, this is Malone. I'm sitting here watching the news and this Water Killer is getting a lot of press. Do you know anything about the case?"

"Yes, the Detective handling the case has called me a few times about it. He has asked me to look into it when I have time."

"Do you think that I could be of any help on the case?"

"Malone, Cirrilo is the Detective of record on this case, will that be a problem?"

There was a long pause, "If it is okay with you, I'd like to talk to him and get back to you."

"No problem let me know what you work out."

"Will do."

Ryan picked up one of the reports that were starting to become a pile on his desk and went through each page making notes in the margins. An hour went by and the pile became a few reports that were still under investigation. His phone began to buzz again and the display read 'Slim.'

"Hello love, what's up?"

"Bill, if you can I would like to see you at my office.

Looking at his watch he replied, "How about I pick up some Chinese?"

"That would be great, see you in about twenty five minutes, okay?"

"Okay, I'll see you then."

He closed the phone and put it in the holder on his belt.

He told Lynn, as he passed her desk, that he would be out to lunch and then be at the Medical Examiner's office if anyone needed him.

It took almost forty minutes for him to pick up the food and get to Rebecca's office. He got thru the access security and found Rebecca sitting at her desk. He leaned over and gave her a kiss and sat in the seat across from her. She looked tired, and when she spoke sounded tired also, she started, "I went over the all of the information in the file you left at the house and it started me looking at the cases of the Jane Doe's in a different way."

Ryan put his hand up saying, "Are we eating here or in the break room?"

She grinned replying, "Here, less distractions."

He stood and started taking the white boxes out of the paper bag and separating the plastic silverware. He placed a plate in front of her and one in front of himself. He looked at her saying, "Go ahead I'm still listening."

She rolled her eyes at him and continued, as he opened the containers and split the food between the two plates. "Well, as I was saying, I looked at the data on the Jane Doe's that I have seen and began to wonder if they could have been surrogate mothers."

Bill had just taken a fork full of food and had to swallow it quickly as to not choke. "Slim, how did you get from a Jane Doe to a surrogate mother? If that was the case than each of the Jane Doe's would be a murder victim."

Rebecca put down her fork and leaning across the desk said, "Right, that would explain there being no evidence of drugs, abuse, absolutely nothing prior to the overdose that killed them. There would be a perfectly healthy child to be sold to the highest bidder or to be used to extort child support payments." She sat back in her chair and just looked at him.

"Slim, I have no idea how you got to where you are, but if they were surrogate mothers. Which is a stretch, how did whoever ran this master scam get the Jane Doe's pregnant with the victim's sperm so that the DNA tests come back positive."

She finished her meal and looking at him replied, "I don't know, that is why we need to meet with your cousin Jerry Patillo."

Ryan finished his lunch and collected the plates and dropped them in Slim's wastebasket saying, "Okay, I'll call Uncle Joe and have him have Jerry call me. I'll ask him to come over the house one night."

She smiled and then almost as a second thought said, "That Attorney that is handling that case against Jerry is the brother of my Professor."

He looked at her and said, "I don't know why, but I do understand that you don't really like your Professor, but are you insinuating that he has something to do with this grand scam you've come up with?"

She did not respond, she got up, and as she walked out of the office said, "I'll see you at home."

He found his own way out and thought to himself, "I've never seen her so abstract."

Chapter 36

ADULLA PUSHED THE FINIAL NUMBER and the phone connected and he could hear the ringing on the other end. It rang seven times before it was answered. He heard, "Day Fishing, Ellai speaking."

"Adulla here, Ellai, is the trip still on schedule?"

"Yes, all is ready, the tides are almost right and the correct amount of bait is close to being collected."

"How much more time must pass?"

"Five days, but no more than six, that is unless something unexpected occurs."

"Fine, what must be must be."

"Adulla, The thing with Kumar that was very bad, very bad."

"He lived like a sinner and died like the pig that he was. He brought shame to his family and they will all pay for his stupidity."

"Yes, you are right they all must pay. The world must see that we do not accept sinners, I will call when it is time to change the world."

"So it will be."

Chapter 37

Barry planned his evening very carefully; this was to be a big night, the biggest. Tonight he was going to do a threefer, yes, a threefer. Let's see if they talk about the damn bag guy after this. He would take the subway uptown to meet the first of the three; he would meet the first just as he leaves his house. He will never mark a tire again, mark tires and cause ridicule. There will be one less rent a cop after tonight and two less some bodies. Who, it did not matter, just so long as they ended up very dead and in a very public way.

Barry dressed for the evening hunt, he put on the replacement boots, socks, pants, shirt, Freezerpac and coat. He had taken everything from the last trip and burned it, he then took the remains and spread them over a half mile of the east river's far bank.

Barry moved out the door with the confidence of a big game hunter, one with a goal. He moved onto the subway train and took a seat on the last car facing forward so he could see all that entered and exited. He watched the stations pass by and he saw everything but looked at nothing. He stepped to the door and waited for it to open. He was starting to get excited, just moments away from one less rent a cop.

The door opened and he moved onto the platform and then to the stairs that led to the street. He climbed the steps and reaching the street level turned and walked across the street to the downtown platform. He looked around the platform and the only person that was present was a policeman. Barry smiled at him, the officer smiled back and turned back towards the tunnel entrance. Barry moved in a roundabout path to come up behind the officer. Just as the officer started to turn towards Barry, Barry thrust the sword upward. The sword entered his left lower chest just under the level of the sternum and traveled all the way up to and through the heart. The officer fell to the platform dead, well before his head hit the platform.

Barry moved away back towards the wall, he stood very still watching the entrance to the platform. He did not know who would enter first, the rent a cop or a stranger but it did not matter. There was a blur of movement at the entrance and Barry hurried to the body. He glanced up and it was the rent a cop, he kept his face turned down and away from the closing officer.

"What is this?" The rent a cop asked as he leaned towards the body.

Barry turned, ramming the sword deep into the chest of the officer. His hand slipped off of the sword's handle and the heel rammed into the officer's chin with such force that it caused Barry extreme pain. Shaking his hand, Barry walked up the stairs and turned downtown. He walked two blocks and then turned east for two blocks to the downtown station. Sitting on the train he inspected his hand and wrist, there was some darkening of the skin on the heel of his hand. His hand felt uncomfortable but he did not feel any restriction of movement. The announcement alerted the riders of the upcoming stop. Barry stood and waited for the doors to open. When they opened he moved across the platform and up the stairs to the street. He turned and moved towards the west side, he walked until he was the only person on the block. He reached under his coat and held the sac and unzipped it with the other hand. A few feet in front of him a door was opening and a young woman stepped out onto the walk.

Barry never missed a step, the sword penetrated her heart and she fell to the walk dead. Barry walked to the corner and turned north and turned left again walking toward the subway station. He was just entering the station when the ambulance screamed by towards his latest victim. Barry smiled to himself, "They will not be talking about any bag people tonight."

Chapter 38

Malone looked at the phone and almost put it down again, but not this time. She pushed the button and heard it connect. It was a second or two then she heard "Cirrilo."

"Cirrilo, this is Malone, don't hang up please, and just listen."

There was a pause then, "Right."

"A lot has happened in the last few days that has changed me, well not me, but what I do. I don't know what happened but I don't constantly hear what everyone is thinking anymore, now I just hear whoever I want to concentrate on. I know that does not sound like a big thing to you but it is, it is a very big thing. Before I was constantly bombarded with information, comments, crap, just constantly. The reason I'm calling is to ask if you need/want any help with the Water Killer Case. Ryan has cleared it if it is okay with you. This is just to work the Case, nothing else."

"Just the Case, okay I'm good with that, but no other crap. Meet me in the morning at my squad room round 9AM and we can go over what I've got so far."

"You got it, see you there." She pushed the 'End' button and scrolled through her stored numbers, getting to the one she wanted pushed the 'Call' button. On the first ring she heard, "Ryan."

"Boss, Malone, I'll be working with Cirrilo on the Water Killer Case starting in the morning. I'll keep you informed as to what is going on."

"Great, be safe."

She pushed the 'End' button and sat there holding her phone and thinking. It had been a while since her last involvement with Cirrilo, they had ended up lovers and it ended badly, he could not handle the fact that she knew everything that he was thinking whenever they were together.

The last few days have been strange she thought, "Most of my life, I've had hundreds of people in my head, and now just me." She was going to have to learn how to deal with people and events all over again.

Chapter 39

*R*YAN PLACED THE PHONE ON the desk and hit the Enter button on his PC. The screen came to life and he pressed the down key and scrolled down to the e-mail he had just received from Cirrilo about the Water Killer Case. He opened it and then forwarded it to Malone with all of the attachments. She now knew as much as he did.

His phone signaled again, "Damn one thing right after another." Picking up the phone he pushed the button and answered "Ryan"

"Hello Ryan," Slim replied.

"Hey, I never looked at the screen, sorry. What's up?"

"I just wanted to call and remind you that tomorrow is the day we need to be up-state in Saint Andrew to meet with Father Thomas. We'll have to leave by six AM to get there on time."

"Oh damn, I forgot about that with all that's going on. Okay, I'll see what I can get set up, this is one of those times I need to be in two places at one time."

"Sorry love, Think we can call Vincent and change the date?"

"I do not think that is an option, I'll just have to make it work. See you at home, love you."

With a smile in her voice she replied "Back at you."

Chapter 40

BARRY PACED BACK AND FORTH across his living space, hands clenched behind him muttering, "No justice, there is just no justice. Fifteen minutes, just fifteen minutes. Three people killed in just hours and all I get is fifteen minutes of news coverage. Damn, a real cop and a rent a cop in the same location at the same time, that alone should have been worth a half hour, Damn, damn, damn."

He walked into the work room and checked his supplies again. He looked in the freezer and counted the swords on hand, twelve swords. He then went to the double door cabinet next to the freezer and ran his hands across the six Freezesacs that hung there. The using of two of them at one time had worked, but it felt uncomfortable and if someone looked at him hard the bulge on one side would be noticeable.

He also worried about some nosey so and so sticking their nose into his business and remarking to the police or news about his very frequent comings and goings. He had to plan his comings and goings better, he needed to stay out longer or find some way to mask his movements.

He knew that one way was to leave later in the evening under the cover of darkness. He had checked and there were only two buildings that had a clear view of his front door and anyone leaving or entering.

One of the first things he needed to do was to put the street light out that stood just twenty-five feet from his door.

He returned to the living area and watched the 48" TV that was replaying all of the four o'clock news. "Damn, its old news, just an hour passed and its old news." He continued to pace.

Stopping suddenly he turned and walked over to the cabinet that stood in the far corner of the living area. He turned the dial on the combination lock and once the hasp hook opened lifted it out of the hasp and pulled the doors open. He moved the hangers to one side and pushed the bottom of the rear panel. It popped outward and grabbing the side edge pulled it behind the hangers.

He looked at the three rifles that stood there in their felt covered slots. He lifted the pump air pellet rifle out of its place and took a plastic box containing the .222 pellets off the upper shelf. He pumped the rifle five times and slid the ammo chamber slot open. He put one of the pellets in the slot and pushed it closed.

He walked over to the front door and opened it as wide as it would go. He glanced out both ways making sure he did not put his head out any further than was necessary. He saw no one in either direction so he took his firing stance and kept the barrel inside the house. He lined up on the streetlight bulb and squeezed off the shot. There was a slight soft pop and the bulb exploded with shards of glass falling into the street. He closed the door quickly but made sure not to slam it. He moved back to the cabinet and replaced the container of pellets and the rifle. In a few moments he had the cabinet back in order and locked.   He moved over to the flat screen and pushed the buttons to switch to the outside cameras that scanned the streets on three sides of the building. There was no movement in any direction. He switched back to the original station. He knew that if someone went through the memory of the controller it would show him scanning the street after the bulb was broken.

Picking up his cell phone and called the Department of Public Works. When the call was answered he began, "Hello, There is a street light that seems to have had its bulb explode. I heard it a few moments ago."

"Right, I'll make a note of it and we'll get to it. Thanks for calling," the line went dead.

Barry laughed to himself they never asked for the address, but he had a recorded call should it ever come up in any investigation. He looked at his watch and a 'Yes' escaped from his lips. He moved into the kitchen area and took a small roast out of the refrigerator and placed the roasting dish in the oven. He set the timer for two and one half hours and set the cooking temperature for three hundred and fifty degrees. He pushed the start button and walked to the work room.

He took one of the Freezesacs and put two swords into it. He hung it over his shoulder and then put his coat on. He checked the full length mirror and saw that everything was in place. He took a prepaid cell phone out of one of the drawers and put it into his pocket. He looked at the small piece of paper from his shirt pocket and programmed the phone number on it into the cell.

He put the paper in his mouth and chewed it for a few moments and swallowed it.

It was time to act, and act he would. To night he would make a statement, one they would really react to. With that he moved towards the door.

Chapter 41

*C*IRRILO PULLED THE CAR INTO the alley and he and Malone got out. Walking towards the rear of the alley Cirrilo said, "This was the location of the first attack, I know that we visited them in reverse but I think it shows the escalation pattern better."

"Your right, this guy is spiraling out of control, it's like he is exploding. Somehow we need to figure out where he is going to hit next."

"The problem is there is no connection between any of these cases. The closest thing we have is two of the dead are Security Officers for the same firm, and they live at different ends of the city."

They walked the path that was suspected to be the path that the Perp had taken. They had walked every inch of every crime scene.

When they got back to the car Malone leaned against the front bumper and looked back at the alley. "Cirrilo, This guy was not very sure of himself when he did this one. Each of the other attacks showed him being more and more forward."

Cirrilo slid into the seat behind the wheel and

replied, "Yes, it seems that he is trying to outdo himself each and every time. That is very scary and not good for anyone."

Malone slid into the front seat and closed the door replying, "Let's hope we can find him before he acts again."

"Right, let's get back to the house and see if anyone came up with anything."

Chapter 42

DANNY PICKED UP HIS PHONE and seeing the call was from Ryan hit the 'Call' button. "Billy, what can I do for you?"

"Danny, I've got to go a few hours upstate in the morning for a meeting. This is something that I cannot refuse to do, no matter what."

"Billy, what the hell, you know that you need to be available at a moment's notice. This thing is way bigger than anything else that could need to be done."

"I'm giving Dutch my 'Vet' tonight and he is staying just ten minutes from the expressway. I will be back in town as soon as I can be, but I have to go."

"Billy, what in the world is so important that you can pass on maybe saving the world as we know it."

"Danny, it's a family thing that I cannot, or will not, not complete. End of story."

"Okay, okay, let's hope nothing happens here. Call me when you get back and maybe you can tell me about it one day."

All he heard was the click on the other end.

Chapter 43

BARRY MOVED DEEPER INTO THE alley on the shadowy side, once he reached the end of the alley he took the cell phone out of his pocket. There was a wooden fence that jutted out from the back of the building about three feet and then it turned towards the adjoining building. He moved into the small space that was protected on two sides but made him invisible unless you went to the back of the alley and turned right. He pushed the 'Send' button and waited for it to connect. He heard, "NBC News, how can I help you?"

"I need to speak to Miss Shara Winters please, it's a family matter."

"Hold, please."

He could not believe that it could be this simple to get through. He heard a beep and, "Shara, who is calling?"

'Shara this is the Water Killer, I know you are recording this and also trying to trace it. I'm going to say this once, if you want to interview me clean up this line and let's talk." He heard her tell someone something and then he heard a buzzing and a clicking then nothing.

"Okay, it's clean, talk to me."

"First, I can see everything that goes in and out of your building, continuously. You and you alone need to exit your building and walk three buildings downtown. Enter the alley and go to the back of it and turn right, I'll contact you then. If anyone else or I hear one car moving too fast, or the blaring of sirens, I'm gone and this never happens. You have five minutes."

"Done, I'm on my way."

He could hear the shaking of anticipation in her voice, this, this was a bluff that he hoped would work just due to the arrogance of the young woman. He could not see anything of her building and he could hardly hear the street at the end of the alley. He was totally at risk, with this move, there was nothing he could do if cops with guns drawn charged down the alley, nothing but die.

He waited and listened it was a few minutes before heard footsteps, high heel footsteps, coming down the alley. He was so ready for her, she turned the corner and stopped suddenly with a surprised look on her face. She did not expect the fence or the sight of the sword entering her chest, and just like that she was dead.

Barry stepped over her and moved down the fence, and when it ended moved down the adjoining alley, and onto the cross street. He did not hear any running footsteps and there were no police cars speeding up and cops with guns drawn.

He turned left at the next cross street and turned right at the next. The CBS news crew was just getting to their van to get to rush over to cover the death of Miss Shara Winters at NBC.

Barry walked across the street and around the rear open doors of the van. Keeping the van between him and the face of the camera on the wall, the most they would have is a few photos of his back. He thrust the sword into the back of the man leaning over digging through a large black bag. He collapsed like wet sack without a sound.

Barry continued walking and turned behind a second van and walked around it and seeing the dead man yelled, "Oh my God, oh my God…. he's dead," at the top of his lungs. People came from everywhere, with all of them yelling, about an ambulance and/or the police. He walked to the street and mingled in with the crowd that was forming quickly. He skirted the crowd until he reached the other side of the street. He moved to the subway station and went in and took the downtown train.

He thought to himself, "Well, I guess I got their attention this time, let's see what's on the Evening News tonight. HA!"

Barry got to the stop before his and got off, he climbed the stairs and walked to the local pizzeria and ordered a salad and an order of baked pasta to go and a drink. Picking the drink off the counter he moved towards the rear of the shop and took a seat facing the front door and the TV.

There were six or seven people scattered around the tables at one stage of eating or another.

Barry made sure that he was noticed by knocking the container of cheese that sat on the table of f, onto the floor. He nodded to each of them for disturbing their meal.

The TV flashed that there was a special announcement. A talking head came on and announced the death of anchor woman Miss Shana Winters at NBC News and the death of Joe Donald, a cameraman at CBS News. These are the most recent killings by the Water Killer. Next the Police Commissioner came on stating that there would be full coverage and every available officer will be on the case. It would be a 24/7 blitz until the killer was caught.

The clerk at the counter called, "Order number one twelve."

Barry walked up to the counter and picked up his order, making sure to leave a larger than normal tip. He walked back to the subway and continued home.

Chapter 44

RYAN MOVED THE CAR INTO the passing lane and increased their speed up to eighty. Rebecca passed him a bagel saying, "Well we should be there about Ten AM, just as Vincent asked, if everything goes the way it should."

"I can get away with running up around ninety five but I don't think this city cruiser will stay together doing that. This is probably the first time it's been over sixty miles an hour. When I kicked it in getting on to the Parkway, it left a long tail of black smoke."

Rebecca grinned, saying, "You have to watch the city dust and rust, and it will take its toll on you."

Ryan looked at her replying with a laugh, "We are still talking about the car aren't we?"

Rebecca rolled her eyes and took a sip out of her Diet Pepsi and grinned saying, "Sure".

The highway made swooping turns around the valleys and mountainsides giving panoramic views of the mountain range, deep valleys and miles and miles of trees. It was nothing like the Rockies but for city people it was pretty impressive.

They had to take the Garden State Parkway, North, to the New York Thruway North, to the 17/6 exchange. Then take 17/6 North to 208 North. They had to continue north until they reached Little Britain Road. Make a right onto Little Britain Road and go thirty nine miles to Saint Andrews. Make a left on Saint Andrews Court and The Church of the Cross would be directly in front of them.

Rebecca talked about the young women that she had processed over the last year that were just ghosts Rebecca had, she had gotten back four responses to her e-mails to the other medical examiners in the surrounding boroughs. Each of them had similar cases that brought the total up to eight perfectly healthy young woman found dead of apparent drug overdoses. Yet none of them showed any signs of the depravation that drug use brought upon the user.

She also discussed her feelings about the information that the file Bill had left on the table contained. She explained how she had done some research and the attorney named in the papers was indeed the brother of her Professor.

This disturbed her a lot, and she explained the reasons to Bill in detail.

He looked at her and truly had never seen her so worked up about something like this.

"You have mentioned to me before that the Attorney and your Professor are brothers and the Jane Doe's might be surrogate mothers, So now are you telling me that you think that your Professor and his brother, a noted attorney, are somehow involved in a plot to kill innocent woman just because they had a baby?'

She looked at him with a stony glance replying, "Are you making fun of me?"

"Rebecca, not at all, but just listen to yourself, if I did not know and respect you, your education and your position I'd think you have read too many dime store mysteries. I promise that when we get back I'll have Jerry come over and we can talk to him and we'll see if there is any way any of this makes sense."

"Fine," she replied with a huff.

The dreaded "Fine" he thought. They rode in silence for another hour and nothing was said until they turned onto Saint Andrews Court.

Rebecca said, almost to herself, "It's so, so beautiful, It's like a painting, a very beautiful painting."

The church was directly in front of them, there were flower gardens on both sides of the walk that led to the main entrance. The flower gardens were so perfect that it looked like someone had painted each of the flowers in each of the beds, the flowers planted on each side of the walk were an identical copy of the other.

"That is impressive," Bill said as he pulled the car around to the side of the church into the parking lot and shut it off. They got out of the car and walked around to the beginning of the walk that would take them to the front doors of the church. Up close the beauty of the flowers was even more impressive.

Just as they reached the church doors one opened and a Priest stood there holding the door open. "Bill and Rebecca Ryan?" He asked with a smile.

They both nodded to the affirmative and walked into the church past the Priest. "Father Thomas," Bill asked as the door closed behind them.

"Yes, yes, welcome to our parish, I have heard many good things about you both from Vincent. Please follow me to the office." With that he started off towards the right side of the vestibule. They followed him and both dipped their hand into the Holy Water and made a sign of the cross as they passed the doors that led to the main church.

Father Thomas took notice but only smiled without making comment.

They reached a open door and entering saw that the room was a small meeting room with a table with six chairs and two more casual chairs that looked like they could be in someone's recreation room. Father Thomas pulled out one of the chairs for Rebecca and he and Bill sat next to her with one on each side.

They were both surprised when he pulled a cell phone out from behind his robe and pushed a button. He then placed the phone in the center of the table saying, "Vincent asked to be called the moment you arrived."

They all heard the phone ring twice before they heard Vincent's voice, "Father Thomas, Billy and Rebecca you are all present?"

Father Thomas replied, "Yes Vincent, we are all here."

'That is good, Billy you have brought the item with you?"

Placing the velvet bag on the table Bill replied, "Yes, I have it right here."

"Please open the bag and hand it to Father Thomas."

Very carefully Bill did as he was requested.

Father Thomas slid the case from the bag saying a prayer as he did so. He held the case with both hands and continual repeated the prayer softly.

"Billy, Rebecca I cannot thank you enough for

bringing the case as I requested with no questions. Father Thomas, please bring in Vincent."

Father Thomas set the case down on the velvet bag reluctantly and stood and moved to the door at the back of the room.

Bill and Rebecca looked at each other with a bewildered look. Rebecca mouthed "Vincent?"

Bill just shrugged.

Father Thomas opened the door and a young boy entered and walked to the table and took a seat. He was a good looking boy but even the most casual glance the observer could tell that he was quite sick.

Father Thomas took his seat and said, "We are all seated Vincent."

"Good, Billy, Rebecca this is my son Vincent, Vincent these are part of your family. They are my most trusted friends and blood."

The boy smiled at them and said "Hello."

His skin was so very pale and a stark contrast to his deep black hair. He was dressed impeccably and sat as properly as one could in a wood chair.

"Father Thomas, would you explain Vincent's present condition please."

"Of course," He looked at Bill and Rebecca saying, "Vincent has been with us for a little over a year. He was sent to us so that he could go through his grammar and high school years as normally as possible. Four months ago he came down with what we all thought was a cold." He looked at Vincent and smiled, continuing "We had the best Doctors brought in and they can find nothing. Whatever it is, it is unknown to the medical profession."

"Billy, this boy is all I have and is everything to me and the future of our family. The object you delivered for me is the one hope that keeps me sane. Father Thomas is going to ask you and Rebecca to assist him with using the case's contents to save my son. I am putting his life in your hands, Father please proceed."

Father Thomas picked up the case and held it out towards the center of the table. He closed his eyes and said, "Bill and Rebecca please place your left hand on the case with mine." They both did as requested. "Now please make the sign of the cross with your right hand and say a Hail Mary at the same time.

The three all performed the actions explained and the case seemed to get warmer. Father Thomas slowly lowered his hand and when he felt the velvet bag on the back of his hand he tilted this hand so that the case would slip onto the bag,

The case slid onto the bag and opened with a pop. A faint mist filled the room and Bill had never felt the feeling of total contentment that he felt at that moment. The four of them sat there looking at the open case, in the center of the velvet lining there was a sliver of what looked like wood. There was a stain on the wood that looked like blood, fresh blood.

Father Thomas took Vincent's hand and separating his index finger placed it on the wood and stain praying in Latin quickly and softly. When he moved Vincent's finger away from the case it closed.

They all just sat there looking at the case and each other. All of a sudden Vincent slumped down in his chair Father Thomas stood and picked him up in one move. As he moved towards the door that Vincent had entered through he said, "It will be alright, I will be right back." And he was gone.

Bill had stood up when Father Thomas had left the room, he sat back down. Looking at Rebecca he said,

"That was something, I don't know what, but it was something special."

Vincent's voice came out of the phone. "Is my boy alright?"

They both moved with a start, they had completely forgot about the phone. Bill answered, "He seemed to faint and Father Thomas took him out of the room. He said Vincent would be alright and he would be right back." Bill looked at Rebecca and continued, "Vincent, what did we just witness."

Before He could respond Father Thomas reentered the room. He spoke with a firm voice, "I believe that I can answer that better than you Vincent."

"Yes, yes of course."

Father Thomas picked up the case and put it back into its case. From out of nowhere a gold clasp appeared around the draw strings. Saying a prayer he placed it in a pocket in his robe. Sitting down he looked at Rebecca and took her hand saying, "Thank you, the true love and compassion you hold in your heart made this wonder occur. There are hundreds of pages that have been written over the past two hundred or so years of the success and failure of the Blessing of the Cross. It has been documented that there have only been eleven instances of the Blessing working over all of that time. It is now, and throughout all time, the belief of the church, and all of its leaders over the past two hundred years, that the gold case is the resting place of a shard of Christ's Cross and the blood on it is his. Let me ask you both a question, the first time you held the case what was your experience?"

Rebecca spoke first, "Well it felt like a warm chill, if that makes any sense."

Bill continued wit, "Yes, it was like a warm breeze that somehow was cold passed over me."

They looked at each other nodding.

Father Thomas smiled replying, "You are both blessed, for I did not feel anything and our ledgers only report that occurrence the eleven times the Blessing Worked.

Vincent, I shall arrange for the case to get back to its place in the Vatican. I will give you daily updates on young Vincent."

"Thank you Father Thomas, Billy, Rebecca anything I have is yours, now and forever. I will be in touch to keep you abreast of my son's health. I know that nothing of today will ever be spoken of again, and the location of my son is safe with you both. God's speed, may he watch over you on your return to your home." The phone went dead.

Father Thomas had moved to the door and walked them to the exit of the church. He took their hands in his and blessed them. Smiling said, "You will always be in my prayers, God Bless."

Bill and Rebecca walked back to their car in silence, Bill opened the door for Rebecca and she got in saying, "Thank you."

He walked around the car and got in, it took just a few moments and they were retracing the trip they had taken earlier that morning. Once on the road Bill glanced at his watch he was surprised to see that they had been in the church for almost two hours. He looked at Rebecca and she glanced back. She said, "Whatever that was it was unbelievable."

Chapter 45

*D*ANNY *AND* D*UTCH* *SAT AT* the table looking across it at the two men they were meeting with. They had been at it for over four hours. The two men were the Assistant Director of the CIA and the Assistant Director of Homeland Security, they had brought well over three years of data, data that had been collected from over one hundred and sixty cities, and thirty five countries, covering the globe.

Once the men were comfortable with Dutch's level five security clearance, their discussions had been long, hard and very direct. A decision had been reached as to the events that would take place, based on the outcome of the actions to recover the shipment of 'Red Mercury' that was on its way to Long Island.

They now had plans and counter plans to meet all of the scenarios that they could think of.

They all knew that this was the biggest threat that faced this county on its own soil ever .Both Assistant Directors had total and complete authority to do whatever was decided that needed to be done. They had all of the might of the United States at their disposal.

There would be no second guessing, no meetings, no second approvals, nothing. Whatever actions that were to be taken, needed to be taken.

The actions would be a true statement of fact.

The men stood and shook hands, nothing but a final nodding of heads and they all left the room without another word spoken but very somber looks on all of them.

Danny pulled the car onto the interstate and pushed it to sixty five in an attempt to get back to the city and then start back home before the rush hour traffic started. He looked over at Dutch saying, "I pray to God that I never have to be part of that kind of meeting again."

Dutch glance back at him replying, "Let's hope that the events that unfold over the next few days prevent these actions from ever having to be repeated, ever again."

They did not speak again until Danny pulled up to the front of the hotel that Dutch was staying at. Dutch opened the door and stepped out onto the sidewalk, turning and leaning back into the car, looked at Danny saying," My very best home cousin." Danny replied, "And mine to you and Janet." Dutch closed the door and walked towards the Hotel's front door. Danny pulled away from the curb spinning the tires a bit, and headed home, he just needed to be home with Maria and the kids for a while.

Chapter 46

_M_ALONE AND CIRRILO SAT ACROSS from each other in the small conference room in his Precinct House. The case files were spread out across the table in no rhyme or reason.

Cirrilo tapped his finger on one of the files saying, "Well we know the Perp is very careful but extremely bold in his actions.

The first attack was on a public subway platform and the victim had to have seen the Perp and yet chose to ignore him. The victim's wound was from the back, so we have to assume that he walked past the Perp feeling no cause for alarm or fear.

The second and third attacks were in concealed areas that were not well lit. He entered through a rear entrance to both buildings.

The first through an unlocked door and the second he broke a glass window pane and reached in and unlocked the door.

The second victim was attacked as she entered the building from the entrance hall.

The third he somehow lured the victim out of

his apartment into the entrance hall. Probably by something he said over the intercom.

The fourth was a homeless man killed in an alley, and there were signs of a struggle of sorts.

The fifth and sixth were again on a public subway platform.

The fifth victim was a New York City Officer on duty. He also was killed from the rear which means he saw the Perp and felt nothing out of order, this allowing him to be taken by total surprise. The sixth victim, from the info found at the scene, was killed as he moved towards the fifth victim to either help or see what his condition was. My question is, what was the Perp doing at that time not to be noticed?

The seventh victim was killed on sidewalk with little or no regard for being seen, she was killed, I believe, just because she was in the wrong place at the wrong time.

The eighth victim was lured into an alley where a meeting was to occur with an exclusive story as the bait.

The ninth was for whatever reason. I cannot think of any reason other than just to kill him.

The worst thing about the entire thing is there is nothing connecting the victims."

Malone pushed a sheet of paper across the table saying, "There are a few things that jump out at me, they are based on the assumption that the weapon is made of ice, if so;

1. How does the Perp keep it concealed?
2. How does the Perp keep it from melting?
3. Where does the Perp get the weapons?

Also

1. Why does no one notice the Perp?
2. Are the victims really random?
3. Is the Perp a man or woman?

Cirrilo picked up the list glanced at it and placing it back on the table and looked at Malone saying, "A woman?"

"Well, it's very possible, from what they are telling me the weapon is so sharp that it would only take eight to ten pounds of force to push it through the chest cavity. A woman could very easily generate that much force to drive it home."

Cirrilo looked down at the table saying, "How is it the ice doesn't shatter with the impact?"

"Well, they are saying that if you freeze water to the temperature of -22 degrees it is at its most dense state and also it's hardest."

"Well, Damn, that opens up the list of possible Perps to ten or twelve million people. With all of them, all twelve million, having access to the materials needed to make the murder weapon." Cirrilo was not using the best tone of voice during their discussions.

Malone seemed not to notice and continued, "I guess so, but I believe that the last two victims were killed to generate a higher level of media coverage. The Perp is in love with seeing the effects that his work is causing on TV, the Internet, and Radio and also in the Newspapers. This leads me to believe that the Perp is a single guy, that works alone or at a job that limits his contact with other people and probably in a closed environment. He lives somewhere that allows him easy access to the subway and the freedom to come and go without his movements being noticed."

Cirrilo put his hands behind his head and looked up at the ceiling saying, "Well, that narrows it down to under a few hundred subway stations in Manhattan and God only knows how many more in the other Boroughs. I guess that's better than the Tri State Area."

Malone, standing, pushed the case papers towards the center of the table and stood there giving him a look of disgust.

He held his hands up over his head saying, "Okay, I'm acting like an ass, and it is totally uncalled for." He put his hands on the table continuing, "Your right with all you said, but we just don't have enough people to stake out all of the subway stations, and if this guy is so normal looking that a cop lets him get the drop on him. How would we spot him anyway?"

Malone leaned over and moved the case papers around until she found the one she wanted. She picked it up and glancing over it almost casually said, "Let's go over the things that we do know as facts, the list of victims. There just has to be something that matches or will lead to a match."

Her cell began to vibrate, she took it out of its holder and pushing the 'call' button said, "Malone."

She heard, "Ryan, all okay?'

"Yes. All okay, thanks," with a grin on her face she pushed the 'end' button and put the cell back in the holder.

She looked at Cirrilo and just said, "Ryan."

With that she moved over to one of the whiteboards that hung on the walls, and wrote out the information that was fact. They had the victim's names, location of the attacks, where they worked and what they did.

NAME	LOC	WORK	JOB
Stan Anderson	Subway Platform	B-Saf★	$ Cop
Karla Harlow	Hallway	EZ Checks	Secretary
John Costa	Hallway	Power of One	Electrician
Jack Brown	Alley	None	None
Allen Wilson	Subway Platform	None	Patrolman
Kenny Samson	Subway Platform	B-Safe★	$ Cop
Cathy Jones	Sidewalk	House Wife	Homemaker
Shara Winters	Alley	NBC News	Journalist
Rusty Jackson	Parking Lot	CBS News	Cameraman

★Worked at High Tech Printing Inc.

They both stood in front of the board, Cirrilo pointed at the list saying, "The first, fifth and sixth all worked in some form of police work, the first a security guard, the second a NYC Police Officer and the sixth was another security guard. Both the first and sixth worked for the same company and at the same off site location. Those three are the only ones that have anything in common."

"Right, we need to find out everything about both of these companies, B-Safe, who they worked for, and High Tech Printing, where they worked. The who, the what, the when and the why of owners, employees, suppliers, everyone and everything. We really need to check whose chops the security guards busted. There always is someone they pick out to prove just how important they are. Also if there are any disgruntled employees or customers."

"Damn, Malone that would mean that the other six people were nothing but collateral damage. That would be cold, very cold."

"No, that means we have a real sick bastard out there."

Malone started to collect all of the papers and files and looking up at Cirrilo said, "I'll surf the Web on the companies, owners and employees. Can you do the same for the security company?"

"Got it, one of the guys that own it is an ex-cop that I know pretty well. I'll see what he gives me first?" With that he started to walk out the door but stopped and looking back at Malone said, "Thanks, I know I started as a Butt and you kept it professional. I think you have us going in the correct direction." With that said he turned and walked out of the room.

A small smile crossed Malone's face, she was very proud of herself. She had not read him once today but handled everything by using her head.

Chapter 47

THERE WAS A KNOCK ON the door and Ryan walked to the door to see who it was. He had a good idea that it was his cousin Jerry Patillo. Jerry had agreed to stop over and review the events that led up to his being hit with a child support case. Ryan opened the door and Jerry said, "Hi."

Ryan replied, "Hi, come on in, Rebecca is in the living room. When they entered the living room Jerry put his hand out to shake Rebecca's hand. She pushed it aside and gave him a polite hug saying, "Were family. Please have a seat"

Jerry sat in the one straight back chair in the room and Rebecca said, "Have a seat on the couch, it's a bit more comfortable than that chair."

Jerry smiled and replied, "Once I got in there I'd never get back out."

Rebecca grinned, saying, "I guess you are a little tall for the couch."

Ryan laughed, "Tall and that isn't half of it. What do you go at? Two fifty?

Jerry replied, "I wish, I'm more like two seventy, I'm bulking up for training camp."

Ryan just shook his head.

Rebecca started, "Well I've read everything in your file and Bill has told me the beliefs that you are living by.

How is it possible that this child has your DNA, if you have never had relations with the mother?"

"I really don't know, but I am being totally honest with you about having sex with this woman or any other one for that matter."

Ryan asked, "Not to be to blunt but have you ever donated sperm for any reason?"

"No Sir."

"Have you ever been involved in any kind of game or competition that involved ejaculating?' Rebecca asked.

Jerry turned bright red and replied, "No I have never done any ..."

Ryan asked, "What did you just remember?"

Jerry rubbed his chin and started, "About ten months ago a bunch of us, guys being recruited by the Pro's, were invited to a party here in the city at the Waldorf Astoria. They gave us rooms and we had a party with all of the food and drinks you could imagine. Well a few of us got really drunk and they had to help us to our rooms. The next day the guys were busting me about my getting my tubes cleaned in the elevator by some good looking blond. I did not remember anything, so I blew it off as just harassment. I've not seen any of those guys since that day. Do you think there could be a connection?"

Ryan responded, "Don't know, but you need to give

me a list of the guys you were with and the date of the party."

"Okay, I'll have to call you with that once I get home,"

Ryan looked at Rebecca and asked, "Do you think it's possible for this to connect to what were looking at?"

She looked at both of them and after a moment or two responded, "I'll have to research that to see if it is possible to collect and store sperm in ….." She was turning a little red herself, "I'll get back to you on that one,"

Ryan and Jerry stood up at the same time and Jerry said, "Thank you, please let me know what is next. I'll call you in about an hour with that information that you requested if that's okay?"

Ryan walked him to the door saying that would be fine.

Jerry stopped at the door and called back saying, "Nice to have met you, thank you and good night."

Rebecca call back, "Night, nice to meet you also."

Ryan walked back into the living room and asked Rebecca with disbelief in his voice, "Is it possible for a person to have oral sex with someone and the sperm be transported in their mouth keeping them alive?"

"I don't know, it doesn't seem possible but I truly don't know. I'll check on that tomorrow and I wish there was a way to see what other paternity suits have been filed." "My bet is none, if there is a scam they would only go after high profile people and they would rather pay then take the chance of a scandal."

The phone rang and Ryan answered it, it was Jerry and he gave him all of the names of the men at the party and also the date of the party.

Chapter 48

REBECCA SAT IN THE CLASSROOM looking at her notes, the Professor was droning on and on about how DNA paternity tests are one hundred percent absolute, He went on about how one cannot be faked and it was imposable to dispute one in a court of law.

She felt that this was a good a time as any to ask one of her questions and to see the reaction. "Raising her hand she asked, "How long would sperm be able to live if in a warm, ninety eight point six degrees F, moist environment?"

He looked a little startled but responded quickly, "At the maximum seven to ten minutes before they would start to stop functioning."

She continued, "What would be needed to extend that time span?"

"Well if the collection is done in s lab, the sperm is flash frozen. In that state it can be maintained for many years. If in a none lab environment, the sperm would have to be contained in some sort of containment device and put on ice as soon as possible. You would then have an hour to an hour and a half to transport it to a location where it could be flash frozen."

She had asked all of the obvious questions, now she needed to ask a direct question. "Professor, could a collection of sperm be collected in a condom during oral sex and then be transported to a lab to be frozen?"

He looked at her for a moment and replied, "Why in the world would anyone want to do that?"

She went for it, "Well then the sperm could be used to inseminate a surrogate mother, in that way it would be able to guarantee a baby would have a certain DNA."

He looked at her for a very long moment and replied, glancing at the entire class, "It seems our Medical Examiner has been reading too many police novels."

The class laughed, but it was almost a forced laugh.

He looked back at her and added, "If you would like to discuss your theory further see me after class and we can set up a time to go over your questions."

She just smiled at him and looked down at her notes replying, "But it is possible to transport sperm in that manner and to complete that procedure to guarantee a baby's DNA, Correct?"

He almost turned away but replied, "Yes."

She watched him very closely for the rest of the class and he was very upset. He gave them a reading assignment for the next class and let them out of class twenty minutes early.

Professor David Stevens was the first person out of the room and by the time Rebecca reached the hallway he was out of sight and headed out of the building.

Rebecca walked out of the front door of the classroom building and into the parking lot next to it.

She was not surprised to see Billy sitting there in one of the unmarked police cars.

He looked at her with a smile and said," It must have been a tough class, the Professor left here like a bat out of hell. I guess you got his attention tonight. Did you discuss anything interesting?"

She laughed replying, "Everything we talked about, oral sex, the condom just everything and he agreed that it was all possible. He responded to each question without a pause, which normally means that the information is fresh in ones mind. I've got it all on the recorder, do you know where he went?"

Graves and Malone are following him, Malone is reading everything that is going through his mind right now. He is headed towards his and his brother's building. I believe that they both are going to get one hell of a surprise in the morning. I've already called the District Attorney and the Medical Board. They both were very interested in what the outcome of tonight's class would be."

Malone repeated everything that she read form Dr. Stevens thoughts, "OH my God, they know about Cathy, Jane, Jones, Sandra, Keisha, Karol, Patty and all of the others. Oh my God, we were so careful, so very careful. It just is not fair, those stupid athletes, all they do is play football, baseball, basket ball. They don't deserve all of that money, not at all. Wait till I get home, maybe we can figure something out. Maybe they don't know and they were just stupid questions from a middle management medical examiner." It went to babbling and Malone stopped reading him.

She looked at Graves and asked, "What do you think, do we have enough for Ryan to get the D.A. to act on this one?"

He looked back and grinning replied, "With Rebecca's smoking gun and the one you are holding, we should have both of them in lock up by noon tomorrow."

They followed the Doctor until he pulled into the underground parking of his building.

Malone asked Graves to pull up to the curb in front of the building. She looked at him saying, "I just want to see how long I can still read him. " She closed her eyes and in a moment began to speak into the microphone of the recorder, "Good, Donald's car is here, we can discuss this tonight. I'm sure he will agree that it is just nonsense, they're civil servants, they could never be smart enough to put all of the different actions and events together to sum up anything." There was a short span of nothing and then, "Donald are you here? Donald? No answer, I guess I was mistaken, and he isn't home yet. Well I gues......

Looking at Graves she said, Lost'em."

Chapter 49

RYAN PUT THE PHONE DOWN and sat there looking at Graves with a smile on his face. He picked up the stack of papers in front of him and looked at Graves and Malone saying, "It took Police One just twenty five minutes to get everyone of these request for search warrants for phone records, bank records, both of their companies files, homes, businesses, cars, hell even their medical files.

All it took was my mentioning that the closing of the case on two brothers, one a nationally known scientist and the other a very well known attorney, could go to Police One, and the Chief, if they just handled the arrest and follow up on the support information, Once they heard both tapes, Rebecca's and Malone's, BAM, they took it hook, line, and sinker. There are twenty police cars, and vans, at that building right now.

We get credit for solving the biggest murder, kidnapping and extortion case in twenty years and they get to do the cleanup. I love it."

Graves and Malone were grinning also and Malone

said, "I hope you are going to take Rebecca out to somewhere very special on the city for this one."

Ryan smiled and replied, "That is a given, the Mayor wants to give her the City's 'Medal for Meritorious Service'."

They both said, "That is great," at the same time.

Malone stood and said, "Well, I'm headed back to Cirrilo's Precinct House. We have a lot of data to go over, photo's, maps, surveys, canvas info, a lot, those guys over there are working 24/7 to come up with something on the Water Killer."

Ryan replied, "Okay. If you think we can help call me."

"You got it Boss, and congratulations again."

"Thanks, but I can only take a small part of that."

Ryan's cell buzzed and he picked it up and hit the call button saying, "Ryan."

"Billy, Danny, We just got a location on the money. They must have had it in an underground vault of some kind. It popped up on the screen and has not moved. We're pretty sure that they are just getting it ready for shipping. It's about fifteen minutes to the closest Long Island Expressway entrance. We still can't do anything but everyone is on high alert and will stay that way until this is over."

Okay, I'm clearing my calendar and heading over to Dutch's room. I'll be there in twenty."

"Got It, I'll call."

Chapter 50

---

*M*ALONE AND *C*IRRILO SAT THERE going over the stacks and stacks of interviews from the canvassing of the three city blocks around High Tech Printing Inc.

There were hundreds of interviews and Malone put her stack down and reached for a different group on papers that was on the employees of both High Tech Printing and the closest neighboring building owned by Data Check LTD.

Cirrilo grinned pointing to the interview sheets and said, "Those get too interesting for you?"

"They're about as interesting as that crap that is on that TV about the arrests of the Doctor and his Attorney brother this morning."

Cirrilo turned and looked at the screen hanging on the wall behind him, "That is all that has been on all day."

Malone looked through the file once and picked out the single men and women that worked in both buildings. She moved over to the map on the wall and put pins in for each employee's home location if it was in the borough. She ended up with seven employees in the borough and three of them within a block of a subway station entrance. She then took the list of the three and compared their interviews to see if anything jumped out. The only thing that just was there was that one of the men had called the city facilities department to report a street light out. With the hundreds of lights out in the city it just jumped out there and lay there.

One of the detectives that worked with Cirrilo walked into the room and stood there looking at the mounds of reports, photos. And assorted papers spread across the table and grinned and just shook his head. As he walked out of the room he pointed at the TV and said, "That is the hundredth time the Chief has been shown going into that building, If you're quick you can catch it on the other three channels if you switch the selector quick."

Malone put the papers she was holding down and looking at Cirrilo said, "Son of a bitch, I bet that the Perp is going to hit again tonight to try and steer the news reports back to him. It has to be killing him that there is not one mention of the killings on any news report. Cirrilo, I think we need to have these three people staked out. Their homes, Cars, everything, we need to know where these three are every moment."

Cirrilo walked over and looked at the names on the list and the locations, "Hell that should be easy to make happen. We just have to make sure we start with where they are now. I'll get our people on the move now." He walked out of the room with the list in his hands.

Chapter 51

---

*B*ARRY HURRIED AROUND THE WORK area collecting everything he would need. He had two Freezesac's on, each with three swords in them. "Take me off the news, huh," well he would show them that that was a very bad move.

He knew where there were a lot of people milling about that included a few dignitaries, time to cull a few. He looked at the clock and from the time it was still light out, "It is time to go, yes, time to go." He walked into the living area and looked at the scanners and saw no one on the street. He walked to the door and opened it and leaned out looking both up and down the street. There was no one on the street and it was bare of any vehicles. He stepped out closing the door and headed across the street to the subway station. In less than fifteen minutes he was on a train heading up town,

Cirrilo pulled the car up to the curb right in front of the door. Malone got out and as she moved around the car stepped on some glass. She looked up and saw that she was standing almost under the street light. She noticed that there was a black mark on the reflector cone that surrounds the bulb when it is in place and increases the coverage of the light when on.

Cirrilo reached the door and pounded on it calling out, "Police." He repeated it again with no response.

Malone looked at him and said, "There is no one in there. If he's our Perp he is out already, out and on a mission. Cirrilo, If I was to take a guess where he would go to make the most impact it would be where all of the News Media has been all day."

He looked at her and replied, "You are right, again by the way, he will be trying to steal the show somehow."

"Well I bet he is going for at least four victims tonight, one better than the last time. Let's get over there, maybe I can scan the crowd and pick him up."

Moving back towards the car he said, "You got it, with the traffic starting it's going to take us forty minutes to get there."

Getting in the car and closing the door she replied, "It is what it is."

Chapter 52

---

*D*UTCH'S PHONE LET OUT A beep and he opened it and pushed the 'Call' Button saying, Dutch."

It's Danny, the money has been moved about a block, I really think that things are about to happen."

"Okay, we need to give them at least a twenty minute head start on the Expressway or the whole chase thing will not work. Have one of the State guys come over and pick up Billy. I'll be waiting down by the Vett for your call. Make sure you tell those State drivers to try and stay two to two and a half car lengths behind me and to keep their sirens going."

"You got it."

He and Billy walked down the stairs, did not need for the elevator to pick this time to act up. When they got to the garage the State car was there waiting. Dutch turned to Billy and said, "Keep them straight cousin." Pointing at the Vett continued with, "We want to bring everything home in one piece."

Ryan grabbed him and with a quick hug said, "We got it."

They both were grinning when Billy got in the car and it pulled away.

As the car started up the ramp to the street the trooper driving asked, "You guys brothers?"

Ryan shook his head to the negative saying, "No, Blood."

Chapter 53

MALONE AND CIRRILO SAT THERE in one of the classic New York traffic jams. Bumper to bumper cars, grid locked in all directions, with a few buses thrown in for good measure. There were three traffic cops trying to get the cars to move so that at least one lane could start to move, if that happened the rest would also begin to break up.

"Do you think we should call and tell the mob that the killer might be heading there way?"

Malone shook her head side to side saying, "I don't think that is a good idea, we don't have a description of the guy and it could cause more confusion and that is what he needs to operate."

The car in front of them began to inch forward, it seemed that things were starting to break up.

Chapter 54

BARRY GOT OFF THE TRAIN and moved up to the street, he set off up town and half a block ahead he saw a patrol officer step into an alley to his right. He did not see another officer or a patrol car. He turned into the alley with his hand down by his zipper. If the cop saw him first it would look like someone had just stepped into the alley to take a piss. The officer was standing at the other end of the alley watching something that was going on back there. Barry moved very slowly and quietly, he was less than two feet from the officer. The officer began to turn around, maybe he felt rather then saw Barry's presence. The sword entered the officer's side and the tip protruded out the other side. He collapsed with a "Suuuuuu," and was dead when he hit the concrete. Barry leaned over the body and looked in the direction that the officer had been looking. There in a first story window was a woman giving a guy a head job. "He deserved to die," Barry muttered as he moved back towards the street.

He walked another block and saw a woman walking alone ahead of him. He increased his pace and in moments he was just a few steps behind her. She stopped and turned around to look at him saying, "Some way I can earn a few dollars?"

He pointed to the alley just ahead and when she took the first step into the alley the sword and its force pushed her a few feet deeper in the alley until she fell dead.

Barry stepped back into the street and continued to walk up town. He was just a few feet away and he heard someone behind him calling for help. It sounded like the officer had been found. He increased his pace a little and crossed the street.

The building he was heading to was two blocks east and three blocks north. The subway stations were much more spread out this far up town.

He felt good, two down and four to go, this would be a night to remember."

Chapter 55

Y HE PHONE HAD BEEPED AND Dutch had it open and the call button pushed in a moment, "Dutch, the money is on the move. We just got a call from the Coast Guard they were just informed by a Navy Sub that a forty foot trawler is moving slowly along the North Western coast of Long Island. They have no lights, silencers on the exhausts and heavy electronic scanning and sending equipment on board. They have the engines and exhausts covered with some kind of heat shields so they cannot be picked up by any heat detection scanners. The sub will be able to track them for another twenty to thirty miles, after that it will be up to the Coast Guard to keep tabs on them.

The money is just entering the Expressway the transport vehicle is traveling at about fifty miles an hour, your show starts in about fifteen minutes. We have the State, County, City and Local Police ready to start the transmitting of the chase in about ten minutes. You should hit the Expressway about five minutes after that, The traffic is heavy so you will have a time setting up to any speed, it will most likely end up a defensive driving show. Good Luck, you go in Ten minutes. This is our last contact, Dutch, Billy will be in the first chase car and the first to reach you no matter what.

"Got it, make sure you get those sons of a bitches in the boat. This needs to end here." With that he turned off the phone and flipped it in the back seat. He got in and started the Vett and pulled it up the ramp to the street. He reached over and turned the police scanner on and tightened his seat belt.

Chapter 56

MALONE AND CIRRILO GOT OUT of the car and started to circle the huge crowd of spectators that the police activity had drawn at the arrest location. The continuous News coverage had made the whole thing a circus.

The report of a slain officer just three blocks away convinced them both that this is where the Perp would be found.

Malone tried her thing not knowing if she could now only scan one person at a time. She looked at a group of about twelve people standing on the opposite corner and opened her mind. As she looked at each one their thoughts came through like a radio station. It was so strange, now she felt like she was eaves dropping on them. Before it just was always there, but now she could single out anyone, anywhere. She looked at Cirrilo and said, "If you see anyone that meets the profile let me know so I can see what their thinking."

"You got it we need to concentrate on singles wearing a long coat."

She nodded as they moved around the crowd that seemed to be increasing.

As they passed a cruiser they heard the report of a second victim being found just three blocks away. "If he is not here he is very close." Malone said touching Cirrilo's sleeve.

He just nodded and continued to scan the crowd for someone that he did not know what they looked like. The two of them continued to move ever so slowly through the mass of people.

Chapter 57

BARRY MOVED BETWEEN THE MASSES of people looking for the next target. He moved outward towards the edge of the crowd hoping he would find a stray. He was hunting much like a Wolf or Mountain Lion would a herd of sheep or cattle. Just keep moving around the outer edge, sooner or later one of the herd would stray. As he got closer to the building itself the crowd was comprised mostly of police officers. Barry looked for the TV cameras and an opportunity to have a culling recorded. It of course could not be the main event but seen in the back ground. He saw a young woman officer moving people back with a little too much enthusiasm. He followed her and sure enough she strayed back about twenty feet from the true edge of the crowd. Ten feet in front of her were two women arguing loudly, about what, who knew. One of the TV crews spun the camera around to get them on film. Barry facing away from the camera slipped a sword out into his hands and in just a moment rammed it into the back of the officer. All taking place on camera and yet without any notice until the officer went down.

As the body hit the pavement a woman screamed and the crowd scattered. There were ten officers there in a moment and yet Barry was slowly moving through the crowd looking for his next victim. He was now consumed with his self imposed quest, he moved like a snake through long grass, His passing left no sign, except the victims that unexpectedly cross his path.

Chapter 58

DUTCH PULLED ONTO THE ENTRANCE ramp at sixty miles an hour. He weaved through the traffic increasing his speed continually. The sirens screamed behind him and there was a flood of flashing lights.

The scanner blared the story of the chase in detail, every close call where a civilian vehicle came close to being taken out, The traffic was all starting to move to the right, either they saw the lights, heard the sirens or just felt the impending doom heading their way.

The chase was being broadcast on all police bands and also all of the Coast Guard bands. Anyone on any type of two way radio was getting the signal. They even had it being broadcast over the CB Channels.

Dutch had the Vett up to ninety-five and was moving around cars that were moving fifty. The driver of the chase vehicle was staying just about two car lengths behind just as planned. He had gotten a signal by the lights on the last over pass that he would be coming up on the money vehicle in about ten minutes. He checked a mile marker as it flew by, he was just where he needed to be and closing fast.

Chapter 59

D*ANNY WAS TALKING TO THE* Commander of the Coast
Guard Cutter that was keeping tabs on the Trawler
that now has picked up speed. It was now moving at
fifty five knots. The Cutter Commander had assured
Danny that they would have men on the trawler within
five minutes of the signal that the other men were in
custody or whatever.

The Sub Commander had also assured Danny that
nothing would get within a thousand feet of the trawler
going in either direction unless they wanted it to. And
it did not matter if it was on the water, under the water
or in the air.

The chase was going pretty much the way they had
thought except the traffic was a lot heavier than they
had expected. They had had five or six close calls with
civilian vehicles that either did not see the lights or
hear the sirens or just chose to ignore them.

Dutch had made a few quick moves with the Vett
traveling around a hundred miles an hour. It was a little
easier for the larger heavier police cruisers to hang in
there.

Chapter 60

*C*IRRILO MOTIONED FOR *M*ALONE TO move to his left, she stepped closer and he said, "The guy in the gray trench coat over by the TV camera. Do you see him?"

She kept looking but the mass of people was really stirring with the death of the police officer. She got a glimpse of a gray coat and concentrated as hard as she could. "Two more and I go home, I will be the breaking news tonight."

She told Cirrilo, "He is over there but I never got a clear look at who I was reading, could be anyone of those ten or eleven people."

Cirrilo charged ahead towards the spot he had seen the trench coat with Malone right behind him.

Malone kept getting short bursts of what was madness. Whoever it was she was reading, was just in front of them. They were moving towards the main entrance to the building and the largest collection of officers. She and Cirrilo moved out of the main crowd and into the area where almost all of the people were in uniform. Malone turned and saw the man with the trench coat moving towards the Assistant Police Commissioner. She yelled, "STOP POLICE!"

A moment later she heard the retort of a police revolver. The trench coat folded and collapsed less than four feet from the Assistant Commissioner. She glanced to her right and Cirrilo was standing there with his revolver at his side. She moved over to him and they both walked up to the body.

The Freezesac lay there next to the body with a sword halfway out of it.

Malone moved it with her foot saying, "That answers a lot of questions."

Chapter 61

*H*E HAD PASSED THE MONEY vehicle almost five minutes ago. He saw the overpass in the distance, the extra lights that had been strung across the tops and on the sides of the railings made it very noticeable if you were looking for them. He saw a break in the traffic so he hit the brakes as hard as he could and put the Vett into a power fade, down shifting when the speed got down to where he could do so without tearing up the transmission or clutch. The Vett slid to a complete stop straddling the entire left traffic lane. The police cruisers slid to a stop with one in front and one in the rear. Three others pulled onto the right hand shoulder. It left a little less than a full traffic lane open.

Two officers jumped out of each car and surrounded the Vett. The announcement of the Vett finally being stopped was blared over every station and band that was available. All of the officers had their guns out and two of them were pushing Dutch onto the hood of the Vett. Traffic had slowed to a crawl just as they had expected. The money vehicle was a new Suburban with blacked out windows, The vehicle could hold up to nine people.

Just as it reached the spot where they were holding
Dutch to the car he kicked the one officer's foot out
and pulled free. He turned and ran as hard as he could
and slammed into the side of the Suburban. The noise
was extremely loud, he did this hoping that it would
cause all in the vehicle to look that way.. At the same
time twelve police officers clambered out of the three
police cruisers parked on the side of the road. One of
the officers chasing Dutch grabbed him, and pulled
him down, almost flat on the road surface.

It sounded like a war was being fought on the
other side of the Suburban, a burst of something big
went off and the windows on both sides of the vehicle
were blown out. The firing continued for another few
moments and it was silent.

Ryan was on the phone with Danny saying, "We got
the money vehicle, get the boat, get the boat!!

Chapter 62

THE COAST GUARD CUTTER COMMANDER yelled, GO, GO, GO, into the microphone. In just moments there were three helicopters with sound deadening blades hovering over the trawler with six men from each on the way down ropes onto the trawler with machine guns at the ready. Less than two hundred feet away a Navy sub rose out of the water with front tubes pointed directly at mid-ships of the trawler. The men on the trawler walked out on deck with their hands in the air grinning. The machine guns fired over a hundred rounds each and most of them found there mark.

The same scene was being played out all across the globe, in over forty countries.

Chapter 63

DUTCH, RYAN AND DANNY WERE all shuttled back to Ryan's Precinct House. They were debriefed and told that they were to discuss any part of the nights events. Doing so would invoke the wrath of Homeland Security.

They had just sat down in Ryan's office when his phone began to buzz, he hit 'call' and said "Ryan,"

Rebecca said, "Get to a TV, this you have to see!"

They all moved into the meeting/conference room and Ryan turned on the forty inch flat screen that hung on the wall.

The Director of Homeland Security stood on a podium with at least a dozen American Flags behind him.

"People of the United States and the world, our local, and military forces have intercepted a shipment of nuclear materials being smuggled into this country by members of aL Queda and fourteen other extremists groups. There were no survivors and no American troops were lost or wounded. As of this moment the following events have been put in motion, under the code name, "OPERATION PAYBACK."

These actions are not anything new, but actions that have been taken by some of our greatest leaders, men such as John Joseph "Black Jack" Pershing, President Harry Truman and President Dwight D. Eisenhower.

In an attempt to provide work and well being for our returning military and the large group of unemployed in our country the following actions will be taken.

Under "OPERATION PAYBACK" the first action to be taken is, All Illegal Immigrants will be deported back to their country of origin. This will be completed over the next twelve to fourteen months. There will be no exceptions and this action will start now. If you are an Illegal Immigrant please report to a deportation station, if you do not you will be hunted down and forcibly removed.

"OPERATION PAYBACK will be swift and decisive."

Anyone attempting to stop this action will be jailed as a traitor and spend up to life in prison, again no exceptions, no trial, just jail. No one is above this law, not our President, Vice-President, all lawyers, judges, police, congressmen or women, senators, news paper reporters, no one. Consider this country to be under Marshall Law, with enforcement by The Department of Homeland Security with support of the United States Military.

Second, The CDI Terrorism Project at the Center for Defense Information has compiled a list of the aL Queda and fourteen other terrorist groups that were involved in the attempt to bring into and explode nuclear grade weapons on United States Soil!

All known members and their support teams have or are in the process of being eliminated.

This action is currently underway in over one hundred and fifty cities in over forty countries.

Any government that attempts to stop this action in any way will be considered offering asylum and allegiance to the terrorists and will be dealt with and acted upon by the United States accordingly. Any country found supporting any one of these groups will lose all aid, of any kind, at once and if Military action is deemed necessary it will be swift.

Again, this action will continue until all members and their support teams of these groups are eliminated completely."

A note to all, a written copy of this data will be in every newspaper in this country tomorrow and repeated every half hour on every radio and TV station, and that includes all of the cable and dish stations.

Chapter 64

BIG FRANK AND SAL SAT at one of the outside tables at 'FLO's' relaxing, reading the paper and making small talk about all that was going on in the family and things in general. A tray of Italian pastries and a full pot of fresh ground coffee sat between them. The pastries were a mixture of their favorites, Sfogliadelle, Cannole and Pignoli Cookies.

They both looked up at the sound of a car door closing and saw Johnny 'The Book' Caprice walking towards them. Three men at different tables slowly stood up with their hands inside of their jackets. Sal watched 'The Book' getting closer and moved his hand from left to right and back. The three men sat down but remained ever diligent.

When 'The Book' reached the table both Sal and Big Frank stood to meet him. The hugged and gave the ceremonial kiss to each cheek.

Sal motioned for 'The Book' to have a seat, a cup of coffee appeared as the three men sat.

Big Frank grinned and said, "You're a long ways from Queens on this fine Sunday morning."

Johnny 'The Book' picked up his cup of coffee and took a sip before responding, "Yes, and it has been a very long time since I've come to visit. I hear that there are many things are happening and what is true or not, I don't know. I came to express my feelings to both of you so there can never be any misunderstanding of where I and my Family stand. My Family and all of its holdings are at your disposal to assist in whatever way needed." He picked up a Pignoli cookie and dunked it in his coffee. He then placed it into his mouth. After he swallowed it he said, "Ah, these must be from Venicro's, they are the best in the city,"

Sal nodded and looking at Big Frank said, "All of what you hear may or may not be true, we will act in whatever way it is decided is best. We have close family involved at the very top and we will not proceed unless asked to be involved. Your offer is heartfelt and will be remembered should there ever be a need. You are a man of honor and we respect you for that."

With that said Johnny 'The Book' stood and took their hands in his and said, OUR God be with you and yours." He turned and walked back to his car, his man held the door open for him and closed it when he was seated. In moments they were gone.

Sal looked at Big Frank and said, "For him to make the trip and say what he did, that is strong."

"Yes, he has always stayed in his territory and always keeps things quite. I do believe that he would do whatever was asked,"

Big Frank pointed at the headlines on the newspaper that sat there and continued, "Over Twenty thousand terrorists and their support teams gone, and over nine hundred million in real estate seized to be put on the auction block to be sold to the highest bidder. A hundred and thirty thousand Illegal's deported, all of this in forty eight hours, and this my friend, is a good thing!"

The both picked up their coffee and toasted each other.